To my two lovely granddaughters
Lauren and Amy
And my wife Edie

A few words from the author

Love and Champagne was originally written and adapted as a Musical, for this reason some of the song's lyrics are in it. It was never performed on stage, but it was done to a private audience, which it received quite a good reaction surprisingly from the few spectators it had, it was well acclaimed, and naturally it was suggested by a couple of journalists who kindly attended, that, if it would never be performed in a theatre, it would certainly be a good story for a book publication. For a start I never thought for a moment to have it as a book format, as my capacities would not allow me to have such pleasure. The musical size of this story with its twenty five new songs and the numerous amount of characters had something to do, by having it been refused by many dramatic societies. I understand shows of this type can cost lots of money to produce, so fortunately I had to be contented to have it published as a book format, I hope that whoever reads it will enjoy as much as I did writing it.

Giuliano Laffranchi

Introduction

Ireland February 1918

Although the first diplomatic call to end World war one came from the President of the United States of America Woodrow Wilson, on the eight of January 1918, that really was the beginning of peace for almost of all the Countries involved in those hatred four years, but that didn't really seem to matter for young Donald O'Reilly, although he spent the last eighteen months of the conflict in simple uniform, luckily without firing a single shot as he was stationed inland to look after various army depositories. He was quite pleased with his position which didn't entail any danger, on the contrary, that gave him enough time to think about his future . So, he had a dream that he had planned for a long time, and that was is gateway to England, at first he thought about New York, but that was more expensive and far away according to his financial status, and naturally a longer journey. Finally, London was the choice.
With the end of the great war everyone was beginning to feel a bit joyful and relieved, of course on the other hand life could be quite unbearable sometimes, difficult and very expensive, especially if you didn't have a job, naturally the black market begun to bite, it was okay for people who had money, unlike poor people, young and jobless like Donald. Anyway, he was not the type to get involved in any mischief, as he would probably land him in trouble, his aim was to look for a bit of fortune and that was a proper job, that's why his ambition was to emigrate. He had heard lots of stories of many people emigrating in the big cities and becoming very fortunate enough to make a little fortune. So he was extremely eager to try and do the same, ready to start from the bottom, as long he could make some money to fulfil his dream. Life was not easy out of the army, he felt the pinch like everyone else, he often thought how much he appreciated during his military service how he was getting almost everything for free, now with great shortage of many things and a very few pennies in his pocket, there wasn't much he could do. But Donald never lost faith, he had the strength of a bull and good brains, especially in maths, and uncompleted school subject that he never forgot, yes, because of the war, he could never finish his studies, he always wanted to become an accountant or perhaps to work in a bank, so he promised to himself that wherever he went he would try to complete such task. While he was waiting for his departure's day, he worked in little jobs here and there, he'd do whatever was on offer, no chance of course to find a full time job, unless you knew the right people, main reason was the religions, politics and in some cases you had to be friendly with the local priest, they almost controlled everything, you had to have some good references to get anywhere, and that was still creating problems for the working class, in other words, you had to be on the right side.

Chapter 1

"London April 1918"

The day arrived for Donald to leave his beloved County Antrim, a beautiful town, a stone throw from Belfast, his parents granted him his wish with some of their savings, with sadness they wished him good luck for his new venture. It wasn't much they could give him as his father was only the bread winner, and sad to say, they probably thought one less mouth to feed. In spite of that his loving mother made sure to put a few extra pounds in his pocket, which she had saved from her part time job as a cleaner, more than anything Donald had to leave behind his friends and the town he loved so much.

It was on a beautiful April sunny day, with an old suitcase containing very few of his belongings, Donald was on his way to his dream. The crossing was rather jumpy as it was quite windy, as the Spring seemed to be late, worse than ever, but he persevered until his feet touched the great Nation he always dreamt about. One long run on the old train and there he was in the great City. Everything looked so big to his eyes, the traffic was unbelievable, he was really amazed to see so many cars, and also a few coaches and horses, he even thought that people had to be very rich to leave in such big houses.

He walked and walked he felt he wanted to see more and more of beautiful London, stopped on the Tower Bridge looking at the small and big trawlers carrying goods and passengers, and very impressed with the Big Ben, he really felt proud of himself to be where he always wanted. Although still sunny, but the afternoon was coming to an end, so he had to think to find some lodgings and then work. What's more than ask someone equal to his class? He was now walking by Charring Cross station, where he noticed quite a few porters;)

"Excuse me sir.....hem.... good afternoon to you!" Muttered Donald to one of the porters.

"Hello me lad, what can I do for you?" Replied the porter. Donald seemed to be blushing:

"Just arrived from Ireland sir, looking for some digs and a job of course, would you be so kind to address me, would you know anywhere, not too expensive please!"

"Hi lad, a job won't be difficult to find, the war has lost so many of our brave good workers! Oh, I know there's the old Metropole Hotel not far from here, they are gasping for staff!" said the porter.
"Thank you sir, I don't mind doing anything that comes along!" Donald replied.
"Go on me lad, go down that road turn on the left and you will see the Metropole Hotel, ask for Mr Jenkins, he's the staff manager and tell him that Jack the porter sent you, I know him well, he's a decent man, he might even put you up for the night" said the porter.
"I am ever so grateful Mr Jack, I feel the happiest man in the world, to have come to London!"
"Good luck me lad, you'll be alright with Mr Jenkins"
"Thanks for the compliment Mr Jack, you are a true gentleman, bye!" And off Donald goes whistling the swinging tune being played by a couple buskers outside the station.

Donald arrives at the front door of the Hotel and ask the doorman;

"Excuse me sir, is there any chance I could see Mr Jenkins?"
"Yes me lad, go right on the back, where you'll see a sign on a door which says; **'Staff and goods entrance'** ring the bell, someone will open the door for you" Replied the doorman
"Many thanks!" Taking his cap off as a polite gesture.

(Mr Jenkins was quite nice to Donald, he could see how well educated he was and reasonably clean, perhaps it was the way he introduced himself. Mr Jenkins offered him a job as a kitchen porter, and knowing that he had nowhere to stay he also put him up for one night in one of the small bedrooms in the top floor;)

"You may start tomorrow morning at seven, and in the afternoon I shall make enquiries for some digs for you, I'm quite certain that we will find something, all I need now is some of your details, then one of the lads will take up stairs to your bedroom, you may also have some dinner tonight, be down here at six, someone will show you the staff dining room, if anyone at the entrance asks you who you are, just say you are a new worker and mention my name, okay? And by the way, tomorrow I will tell you how much we will pay you, your working hours they will be on the kitchen rota notice board!"

"Many thanks Mr Jenkins, I am ever so grateful, I promise I won't let you down!"

Donald was taken to his small bedroom, it was very clean and to his surprise there was a bath next door, that didn't stopped him to take a chance and have a good wash, he really felt great after and with an hour or so before dinner he ventured out for a walk making sure to be back in time for his free supper. The staff dining room was huge, and quite clean, the staff were of different colours and numerous, but that didn't seem to matter to Donald, in fact he was feeling quite at ease there were two cooks dishing out the food, and the portions were almost too generous. Donald was very hungry, the food was good, he really enjoyed his beef stew with dumplings, a second cuppa and a little chat with some of the workers. After dinner he went up to his room and decided to write down in his small booklet his first adventurous day in London town.

Next morning, seven am. Donald made his appearance in the vast kitchen where he was shown and told what to do, the staff were quite friendly and made him feel at ease, although everyone seemed to work without too much nattering, and very soon he got to know how to wash up dishes, the only problem it was with that kind of caustic soda that left some white marks on his hands, at first he became worried, but one of his colleagues Tom reassured him that his hands would become normal soon after.

"Yes Donald, I wouldn't worry about the state of your hands, in twenty minutes or so, they'll be back to normality!"
"Oh, thank you Tom, I was really getting worried about that!"
During his first lunch break he sat next to his new mate Tom, and as the conversation went on, Donald mentioned that he was looking for somewhere to stay, explaining that Mr Jenkins was kind enough to put him up for his first night, but promised to him help to find digs.
"Mr Jenkins never comes around before lunch, as he has a lot of paper work to sort out in his office, but rest assured you'll see him before we take our afternoon break!"
"Oh, I hope I will as I am rather worried about finding digs!"
"Haw.... wait a moment Donald, I just remember; Yesterday I saw a notice in a corner shop window advertising for a vacant bedroom, it must be above the shop!" Said Tom.

"Oh, jolly good Tom, is it very far?"
"No, it's not very far, it's around the Paddington district, if you are interested I'll take you there this afternoon, we can catch the old bus, it will only take fifteen minutes!"
"Oh, that would be great Tom!"
"No problems my friend, I know what it's like to be without digs, I went through that myself!"
"I do appreciate that Tom, in the meantime I shall have to let Mr Jenkins know that I might have somewhere to stay!"
Donald saw Mr Jenkins before he finished his shift.
"Thank you Donald, I am pleased to hear it, and please if you don't find it, do come back to me as I might have some addresses to somewhere else!"
"I will Mr Jenkins, and thank you very much for your concern!"
As soon as they finished their shift, Tom took Donald to the corner shop where he saw the advert. It was a small house right on the corner of one of the sides streets of Paddington long road. The owner introduced himself as Mr Ryan, and so did the two boys, naturally he seemed to be pleased to meet Donald knowing that they both came from the same Country.
"Nice to meet you boys, Yes the room is available, I presume is for you Donald!"
"Yes Mr Ryan, I just started my new job at the Hotel Metropole, and I do need somewhere to stay, is the room very far from here?"
"Not at all Donald, just above this premises, which belong to us, if you like the room, it'll cost you two shillings and six pence per month in advance, if you'd like to see it, I will call my wife, and if you like it, you can arrange with her to move in whenever, even today!"
"That'll be great Mr Ryan, I am sure the room is okay, if you don't mind I can move in this afternoon!"
"Good Lord, you are desperate my lad, that's fine by me. Oh, by the way, you'll have to use the front entrance when you come and go, and if the shop is shut, all you have to do, is ring the bell and we will let you in, in any case, we are open all hours, in the meantime I'll leave you to arrange the rest with my wife, she's in charge, like all women, mind you I've got enough on my plate as it is!"

(Donald met Mr Ryan's wife, a very charming lady with a pretty face, blue eyes and very chatty as she wanted to know many things about

Ireland, she and her Husband had not been there for quite a few years, for all sorts of reasons, the main one was the war, and of course the shop. They had a daughter called Mary Louise, now seventeen years old and still at school.)

"We care so much for little darling, yes, we really want her to learn a proper profession!"
"Yes I do understand Mrs Ryan, I know the feeling, as for myself I could never complete my studies because I had to do my duty for the Country but I'm hoping to regain what I've lost!"
"Oh yes? Which profession were you studying for... if I may ask?"
"Well...... I always wanted to become an accountant, and it still my intention to pick up where I left off, once I'm settled and with earning a few pounds, I think I'm pretty good with my maths!"
"I like your goodwill and determination to get somewhere Donald!"
"Please may I ask you and Mr Ryan to address me as Don?"
"Of course my dear, Don is so much up to date....ha, ha, ha, ha!"
"You are so right to laugh Mrs Ryan, Donald is such an old fashioned name!"
"No, your name is not old fashioned my dear boy, you should be proud of it, as it is the first best present that your parents gave you!"
"Yes Mrs Ryan, you are right, I know for a fact that it was my mother's choice! In fact my grad father was called Donald!"
"See.... I was right then.... Don, you should be proud to carry your grandfather's name!"
"Indeed I do Mrs Ryan and I thank you for your good words, if you allow me I'd like to say that you just sound just like my mother!"
"Thank you for the compliment... Don!"
"It's me really that I should thank you! Now I shall go back to the Hotel, to pick up my few belongings, in the meantime here's my two shillings and six pence in advance!"
"Thank you Don, I shall give you a receipt when you return, no need to rush!"
"See you later Mrs Ryan!"

(Don was ever so grateful to Tom for helping him to find such friendly people, on the way to the Hotel, they seem to have acquired for each other true friendship.)

"Thank you Tom, for your kindness more than anything, for taking the trouble to take me to the Ryans, it's very much appreciated!"
"Don't mention it Donald, you probably would have done the same in my place!"
"Yes, I suppose you are right, and please you may call me Don too, and tell me Tom, what is your full name, which town do you come from?"
"Well, my name is Thomas Wilson and I come from Liverpool, I'll be honest with you Don, I don't particularly like London that much, I prefer my Liverpool!"
"Why did you come down here then?"
"That's easy my friend, there are more people out of work in Liverpool than in the all of London!"
"That might be so, think of it Tom, London can give you a lot of opportunities to make a few bobs!"
"Yeah, you might be right Don, provided you are clever enough to look for them!"
"All you need it's some goodwill and determination!"
"I suppose you are right Don, I'll think about it!"
"That's what I like to hear my friend!"

Chapter 2

(Back at the Hotel. Don put together his few belongings in his old suitcase, caught the old bus and moved in with the Ryans.)

"Hello dear boy, that was quick, please go through, Mrs Ryan is on back room stacking up some of our deliveries, my young daughter is helping her!"
"Thank you Mr Ryan......"
"Oh.... hello Don, I will take you up to your room in a jiffy, by the way, please meet our sweetheart Mary Louise, she's just back from the college, as you can see we all work here, she's giving me a hand with these goods, and later she'll have to do her home work, ain't that right Louise?
"Yes Mum! So, you are Don, well.... nice to meet you, my name is Mary Louise!"
"True, I am Don! Nice to meet you too Mary Louise!
"You can carry on Louise, while I take Don up to his room!"
"Okay mother!"
"She's so good, very caring and very hard working, she always wants to help in the shop when she's not at school!"
"I can see that Mrs Ryan, that's what I used to do with my parents, when I wasn't at work!"
"Well, I must be honest, very few children grow up like that now days, I think I blame the parents, they spoil them rotten!"
"Maybe you are right Mrs Ryan, but I think this is only happened with the well off families!"
"You've got a point there Donald. There you are, this is your room, it's not very big, but very comfortable, as you can see you also have a little table and a chair, I also put you a couple of towels, just in case you don't have any, you can use the bathroom on the second floor, mind you that's the only one we have."
"Thank you Mrs Ryan, maybe I will buy some towels as soon as I settle with my new job, the wages are not very high but I get my food free, which is something, that will help me to save a few pennies."
"Don't worry about buying the towels, I've got plenty, you just think of settling in, we know what is like emigrating to a new Country, we went through the same, times were more harder then!"

"So I gather Mrs Ryan, life it's not so easy in our Country either at the moment, times are hard everywhere, sadly we can only blame that nasty war!"
"Don't tell me Donald... we know the feeling, but with our little shop, we are slowly picking up the losses, and so we can provide good education to our sweetheart!"
"That's the main thing Mrs Ryan, good education is very important, it's a great advantage to get on in life!"
"Yes, we would like her to become a lawyer, to know the law in life it's very important too, apart from the fact that some laws are not very fair to people like us, however I shall leave you, for now!"
"That's true Mrs Ryan, like the old saying; don't do as I do, but do as I say. Thank you a Mrs Ryan for your great help, is greatly appreciated!"
"I like that saying, it does make sense, and very pleased to help you!"

(Mrs Ryan went back with her daughter carrying on stacking the shelves)

"He seems quite a nice lad that Donald, what's your impression Louise?"
"Yes mum, I think he's a very nice boy, and by the sound of it, he's very well educated, you can see from his behaviour!"
"I agree with Louise, certainly not like some of your school mates, most of them are very spoiled, perhaps by their parents, I suppose!"
"Oh... mum, I think sometimes you are exaggerating, they are not all that bad, you have to think that we are the new generation, and so we are slightly different than old generation!"
"Don't we know we are getting old..... ah, ah, ah, I suppose a little laugh is good to our health!"
"Yes mum... I think you are right, you just got to laugh sometimes, you can't change the world!"

Don and Mary Louise seemed to have become quite friendly. Perhaps it was Louise trying to make Don feel at ease, plus for the fact that Don started to help her out with her school home work as he found it very easy for him, considering his good knowledge of English grammar and maths, she seemed to appreciate his help a lot, she certainly didn't get any help from her parents, they were too busy running the shop, somehow her father didn't seem to like that kind of close friendship as he knew well, although only seventeen, she was now a good looking young lady, but daddy always called her 'my little princess, they did keep their eyes on her quite a lot, in spite of that, the Ryans became fond of Don, as some afternoons during his few hours break from his job he used to help out in the shop or help some old ladies home with their shopping. Sometimes the parents even asked Don to go and fetch her from college, as Mr Ryan always thought the worse, of the other half of people walking around London, on this instance, he probably thought that Don was a good body guard. Don was treated almost like their own son, every afternoons, there was the usual cup of tea with a few biscuits. Six months went by. Although he was spending two afternoons a week in a school in Oxford Street trying to pick up what he left off from his old college studies for his accountancy diploma, at the same time, he was also getting his experience with keeping the Ryans accounts in order he was quite good at that. Don was starting to get fed up with his job as a kitchen porter, it was getting him down, it was not that kind of profession that he dreamt of, but as he had no choice he persevered with his Hotel job, with full dedication. Plus he lost his good friend Tom. Yes, Tom had to go back to Liverpool as there was some problems in his family, however, they promised each other to keep in touch but after a few letters their beautiful friendship died off.

Two months later

Don carried on with his school and finally he was awarded the long waited diploma of accountancy. So now he was ready to try his experience with a firm, even though he knew he had to start from the bottom.

One day he saw an advert for a job he was looking for, some kind of gold opportunity for him, he thought, which was to assist the accounts department of a big company, and that was a chance he couldn't miss. With plenty of courage he applied and to his surprise he got the job. Before anything else he had to find digs near his new job which it was just outside London. Once again he was lucky to find digs near his new job, it was in a house owned by Mrs Crosby a widow, having lost her husband, it looked as though she was delighted to rent him the room which was self contained with a private bathroom, she was pleased to hear where he was going to work, as her late husband did work there for quite a few years, that made Don's situation easier, and more homely. not only that but she told Don that her husband was very friendly with Mr Willis the Managing Director. That made Don very pleased to hear some details of the firm before he started his job.

(Next it was to approach Mr Jenkins, and explain the situation of his new job, of course, that was not a problem he was more than pleased:)

"Oh I am so pleased for you Donald, I think you deserve some kind of a better opportunity in life, you are clever enough, and don't bother about a week notice, when you are ready to go you are free to do it, just tell me the day before, I'll have no problems to replace your Job, that's for certain. You have been a good worker!"
"Thank you Mr Jenkins, I shall never forget what you have done for me, when I was desperate for help and I did appreciate your kindness to put me up for one night!"
"Don't mention it my lad, I can only wish you good luck, as I said, don't forget to give me at least a day!"
"No problem sir, and thank you again for your kindness!"

Chapter 3

"Now.....The time arrived to delivering the news to the Ryans," said to Don to himself, "that it's not going to be easy, but I am sure they'll understand." In fact that is exactly what happened. Mr and Mrs Ryan were quite sympathetic and they were quite pleased to hear that I had gained his diploma of accountancy. he also told them that he would vacate the room the next day, as he had to start his new job as soon as possible, he apologized for not being able to give them at least a couple of weeks notice. Mary Louise was not there she was staying with a school friend for a couple nights, so he was unable to say goodbye, he really felt sad, as they had some wonderful days together, laughing, and joking, plus a few times they went to the cinema, naturally with her father's permission, he could see she was always so happy to see him around, especially when he used to pick her up from her college now and then, she was somehow so proud to introduce him to her school mates, although, she never mentioned to anyone that he was a kitchen porter, he was not ashamed of that, never the less, she did say to everyone that he was studying at a college in Oxford street, which he was in all fairness true, but only for fifteen hours a week, at the same time he did appreciate the way she thought of him, in other words it doesn't matter what you do, but it does matter who you are...........)

Donald started his new job with a big oil company called 'Liquid Gold & Co`. Don was very pleased with his new lodgings as he had all the facilities he required. His new job was in the financial department, where he was more or less checking the ins and out of the company expenditures. With the help of his personal secretary Elizabeth Campbell he seemed to pick his job very easy, more easier than he ever thought. A vacancy became available and being so good at his job, he was made head of his department. Few years later he became one of the Directors attending regular business meetings. For he had become the protégée of Mr Willis the Chairman To get to this stage he worked very hard and very long hours and his job gave him quite a few remunerations, plus he had the chance to get involve in shares, making the company better off than it was, and allowed him to buy company shares too at a fair price. Things were looking up. Sadly his landlady, Mrs Crosby could not keep her house any longer as she was too frail, she offered Don to buy it. So he did, but as time went by he realized that was too big for him. Elizabeth suggested that he should get a small bungalow and keep the house for his family for whenever they would come visit him.)

"There is one for sale next to mine Don, I think you should go and see it, it has lots of good fixtures, large garden and three large bedrooms, which one you could make it into an office, as you always take home accountancy work to do!"
"That sounds a good idea Elizabeth, can you make arrangements for me to see it?"
"When would you like to go?"
"How do I know.......? You have my diary, you can choose the day, in fact I would like you to come with me that day then we could go out for a meal as a token of thanks for your kind help, and naturally to celebrate my new property!"
"You mean you already decided to buy it?"
"Why not, properties are a becoming good investments now days."
"By the way, can you book me a crossing to Ireland in a couple of weeks, make sure to make the return no more than three to five days!"
"Why so short Don, you haven't seen your families for a few months!"
"Elizabeth..... I really haven't got too much time to spear, therefore I like to see this bungalow as soon as possible. and don't forget to book a table at the usual restaurant!"
"It will be done sir, I am quite sure that you will like that property!"
"How many times have I told not to call me sir? Yes, after that you'll have to arrange for a surveyor, must make sure that it won't fall apart or sink in the ground!"
"No chance of that, the building is sitting on higher ground."
"We must take all precautions Elizabeth!"

Elizabeth was very attractive, single and with no boy-friends. Don knew how Elizabeth felt about him, but he had no intention of getting tight up, some people even thought that he wasn't interested in women, and yet he was always charming with them, especially with Elizabeth, sometimes he treated her better than anyone else, so they were just good friends.
Don was looking forward to go and see his family, unfortunately it didn't work out like that, because with great sadness news suddenly arrived for the loss of his father, so within a week he was in Ireland

comforting his mother. The good thing was that he could look after his mother financially more than his brother and sister, of course they had families to feed, but they were always there to see that mum was reasonably well looked after. Don returned to England after a week, to sort out the bungalow business, but to his surprise Elizabeth did everything to his satisfaction, all he did, was to sign the buying deeds.

"Thank you Elizabeth, I am so proud of you, I just cannot express it in words!"
"That's what a secretary is supposed to do Don!"
"Yes, yes, I know, but you do more than that, I really do appreciate that, however, it was nice to see my family, considering the sad situation they are in."
"I am so sorry to hear that Don, I know the feelings, it was a sad time for me too, when I lost my parents within a year, I certainly did not expect that!"
"Well, these are the facts of life, and sadly we can't get away from them!
"True Don, we must take life with a pinch of salt sometime, and try to enjoy yourself a bit more, we don't really know what's around the corner!"
"Yes, I agree with you on that..... Do you think you could find me a firm who could make my bigger house decent for my lot, I think they will come and visit me soon, that is after I move in the bungalow."
"That's no problem Don, I know the right people that can do the right job!"
"Also I might need a builder and a plumber Elizabeth, after this we shall go together to buy what we need, I want to make my family comfortable especially my mother, she almost never had any decent holidays!"
"I admire your love and dedication to your family Don!"
"That's the least I can do for them, I am sure they would do the same for me!"

(Don always kept in touch with his family, but again before he could have his mother in England, news came that she passed away all of a sudden, once again he went back to Ireland, for a week or so. This time he was thinking what Elizabeth said; that life should be to enjoyed more.)

"Perhaps Elizabeth is right, she told me this numerous times!" Don was talking to himself this time.
But back to the drawing board, Don never exceeded his humble living, this was one of the best thing he treasured as he never forgot his roots. He often thought that he needed to settle down, because he was not very far from his forties, but apart from Elizabeth, he didn't like any others, if he had to choose, it was her. Yet he was not that convinced 'My God she's beautiful!' He thought. Yet, for some reasons he could not make up his mind, something stopped him, hoping very soon he would make the right decision.)

Chapter 4

(Naturally the roaring twenties which brought great economy growth and prosperity by a recovery from war time devastation, although that long recession caused by World war one was still felt many years after and with the great collapse of the world monetary banks in nineteen twenty nine, recession was still hanging on in some Countries. Don's job was now in its fourteenth years anniversary and getting better and better, but that took a lot out of Don's brains, so to speak. Some days he was getting depressed as he felt like wanting a change of his daily routine. One morning after his weekly meetings, he was ask by his Chairman Mr Willis, to stay a little longer as he had something to discussed. Mr Willis was the top man and thought the world of Don.)

"Well, well Donald, I think he could be healthy and wise for you and me to have a little chat now and then, we never have chance, all we seem to do is talking money! Right?"

"That's how it is when you are in business sir, never the less it's nice of you to ask me. I am overwhelmed, but please I rather if you address me as Don as everyone else!"
"Nonsense Donald, you know very well that I address my staff by their surname, and you are the only one that I call you by your name, actually I like it, one of my cousins is called Donald and I think is a bloody good name, if I may say so!"
"I am pleased to hear that sir, and may I add that my grandfather was also a Donald!"
"You should be proud of it then! Well..... now and then a little bird told me that you look and feel rather tired and depressed these days, I know you lost your parents within a short period or maybe it's your job, giving you too much stress, so, I think a good break would do you the world of good, I suggest that you go and pack your bags and go to Paris for a long week, take a friend with you or a girl friend if you have one, why not Miss Campbell? I am sure she wouldn't refuse, you only have to smile at her and she'll do anything for you, she's a damn good girl. Naturally, all expenses will be paid by the firm and you may stay at the hotel the Paris, as we have an account with them, therefore you won't need to take too much cash!"

"Well... that's very kind of you sir, perhaps I will, and I am sure Elizabeth, I mean Miss Campbell would be delighted to join me!

"Damn it Donald I'm sure she will, that girl will follow you without saying a word, and there's no perhaps or maybe.... go and pack your bags and have a good time!"

"Thank you sir.... I don't really know what to say!"

"Say nothing.... go and enjoy yourself, I only wish I was young like you... Bye Donald.... send me card of the tour Eiffel, or maybe one from the Moulin Rouge, I hear they have beautiful dancers there!"

(Don sat at his desk and kept thinking the best way to ask Elizabeth, he was more afraid to hear her say; Thank you but I can't, what else would she say? Thinking they only had lunches and dinners together but with clients, and of course the occasional dinner of appreciation, yes he did invite her at his place now and then, and so she did too..... but not being on our own in a hotel, she's such a lovely girl, he knew he wouldn't hurt her feelings not in a million years, never the less.....he thought he had to ask her, further more what Mr Willis would think, if I declined his offer? Anyway, he did fancy a trip to Paris, knew some history about it, as he never seen it before. So..... Don gets up from his desk open the door and.....)

"Hello Elizabeth, can you come in to my office please?"

"Right away Don, shall I take my note pad?"

"No, just yourself!"

(Five minutes went by and no sign of Elizabeth, I found that very odd, but all of a sudden....)

"Sorry Don, I had to go and wash my hands from some nasty ink!"

"Not to worry Elizabeth, please take a seat!"

"Thank you Don!"

"Well... I don't know how to say this..... I promised I won't be offended if you say no!"

"Well, for a minute I thought I was getting the sack....." **(said Elizabeth laughingly)**

"Oh nothing like that..... I've just been told by our chairman that I should take a week off, mind you more like an order, you know what he's like, when he wants something done!"

"Please don't tell me, I know him well!"

"Yes... he suggested that I should go to Paris to relax my mind, so to speak, he also suggested that I could take a friend, I thought about you, I like the idea and quite honestly I don't really feel like to go on my own, well.... how about that then? Would you be so kind to join me? Let me assure that this is not a catch of some sort, we are going there just like two happy friends!"

"Don I'll be more than delighted, but I am not sure whether I'll be able to afford my own way!"

"Ehm.... Don't worry about that, the firm will pay for everything, and if anything you deserve a break too!"

"Oh, Don I always dreamt to go to Paris, I read so much about it, is it a dream?"

"NO, it's not a dream.....today is Friday, and tomorrow I will make all the arrangements, this time I'll be the secretary, and early Monday morning we shall meet at Victoria station where we shall head to Dover to catch a ferry to Calais, from there we shall proceed to Paris by train, you've got my phone number, just give me a ring tomorrow, luckily I'll be able to give you more details!"

"Oh Don.... I am so exited, I just can't believe it, is not a joke, is it?

"Would I joke about things like that Elizabeth? I am so glad you accompanying me, I'm sure we'll have a great time... go on now, I have a lot to organize, I am not as good as you know?

"Thank you Don.... see you then at Victoria station....bye!"

(As arranged, they met at Victoria station on Monday morning, although they managed to catch an early train to Dover, they arrived at eleven am, the sea looked so calm and smooth, they were able to board the ferry at twelve noon. The crossing was very pleasant, but it seems to take ages, what a beautiful scenery that was when they watch the white cliffs of Dover fading away. Just in time to catch the train direct to Paris, but, alas it stopped at every station, in the end it was quite a nice trip, enjoying the French countryside, they had very little to discussed though, they tried to avoid the subject WORK, they were going on holidays, that was their destination, so to speak, exchanging some memories when they were kids. Yes they were lucky to be treated to a such luxurious holiday. They arrived in Paris at six pm and caught a taxi to the hotel the Paris.)

Chapter 5

"Here we are Elizabeth, this is a bit different than London don't you think?

"Goodness me, it certainly is..... and very impressive too, what a beautiful entrance.... Oh, this is really glorious! Are you sure you have the right place?

"Of course I'm sure dear.... I've got the letter here of introduction for the reservation. Glad you like it Elizabeth, and here we must make the best of it, this is our chairman's choice, I suppose he has been staying here quite a few times!"

"I believe that ... and.... Well.... I am speechless Don!"

"When the hotel was booked I specifically said that I required two bedrooms, I asked for two singles Elizabeth.... ehm... I thought next to each other, I thought I could be your body guard too, I already notice some masculine's eyes looking at you, of course you deserve that, as you are very attractive.. and beautiful, if I may say so"

"Thank you Don... you are too kind, but I am not interested in anyone looking at me, I am quite happy to be with a good looking man, if I may say so; that one is you!"

"Well... I think I'm going to blush, that's very kind of you Elizabeth, oh, I also booked a table for two at eight thirty in the main restaurant, if it's alright with you, I thought we'll have plenty time to freshen up without rushing too much!"

"Fine darling, sorry Don, this just came out without thinking!"

"No problem Elizabeth, say what you feel, we are not at work now, let's catch a lift and go and get ready, our suitcases are already in our bedrooms....(**Arrived in front of their doors).** here we are, make sure you've everything you need, if you need anything please let me know, just knock on the door, the bedrooms are connected but there are two locks, one for each of us to lock and open, I will ring the reception, in the meantime I'll see you in the main bar... say; forty five minutes, for a cocktail! Okay with you?"

"That's plenty time Don... see you in the bar!"

(In the bar)

"Hello Elizabeth, you look absolutely radiant, just the girl I would take out to a nice restaurant..... Like that one, **(Pointing at the restaurant quite near to the bar)** hem....sorry to be late, I was on the phone to our chairman, actually he rung me to make sure we got here alright..... By the way, he sends his regards to you!"

"Hope you thanked him for me, he really cares about you that man, well, I suppose he will not find any other loyal than you. thank you for your compliments. Goodness me, there seem to be quite a lot of people staying at this Hotel and you pointed out I can see the restaurant from here, it looks very beautiful......That is a change from our usual one, mind you I heard many times that France or I should say Paris is very well known for their restaurants or let me refrain that, culinary ambiance. "

"Goodness me, you did say that already you seem to be well acquainted the French culinary ambiance....Yes it is a beautiful place, but I presume people who comes here a lot, do not appreciate good things like us. Talking about our Chairman, he knows too that you are not only wonderful but a perfect secretary for his firm and as for myself, I'm only only trying to do my job properly, of course without your help I couldn't do it as good. Please no comments, now then let's order a cocktail.

"Nothing too strong Don!"

"May I suggest a Champagne cocktail, I had it before and it's not very strong!"

"What's it got in it?

"Obviously Champagne with a touch of; gin, maraschino, kirsh and French vermouth, it is superb!"

"Go on then, when in France do as the French do!"

"That's my girl...... Garcon **(calls the waiter)**

"Oui monsieur...."

"Deux Champagne cocktail sil vous plait!"

"I didnt know you spoke French Don..."

"Just a few words, learnt in school, Oh, I'll have to order a bottle of wine with our dinner, what would you like, Elizabeth?"

"OH.... I am easy, I'm not really a connoisseur, but I like a glass of wine now and then!"

"That's fine then, may suggest a nice bottle of Pouilly Fume', it will be okay with the Langoustines, that's kind of large prawns.... actually they are from the lobster family! Do you like them?"

"That's very interesting, I like fish, any kind of fish, and how do you know they have these Langoustines?"

"I saw them on the menu, on the door's restaurant when we arrived."

"You are very observant Don, I must say!"

"Then it is Poully Fume', I like it nice and chilled!"

"I am just following you Don, just relying on your good knowledge, I presume you learnt this entertaining our customers!"
"Most of it, I must admit.... well, here they are our cocktails, cheers darling! May I call you that too, as we are not on duty now? Oh, you must try a couple of those canapé, they look very appetizing darling, try the vol-ou-vent with mushrooms they are superb, and also the caviar ones!'"
"Actually I feel more at ease if you call me darling, and I am delighted to hear it, I just see in you a new Don, if may say so..... OH, these canapé are superb, they just compliment my cocktail."
"They are very tasty indeed! You might be right, I do feel like a new man, that is being away from that desk, which always filled my mind with figures!"
" True Don, that desk only allowed you to smile once a day!"
"Maybe once a week Elizabeth, never mind...... Oh, here we are in Paris at last, I think we should make the best every day of our stay, as it is our very first time in this loving City. I'm going to order the wine, I won't be long."
"Take your time Don, we have all evening!"
"Okay that's done, I was told that the wine is at the right temperature, also our table is ready, so we might as well make our way in, but please, let us finish our cocktail!"
(Their food arrived quite at their leisure, and they seemed to have enjoyed it immensely.)
"Would like a coffee Elizabeth?"
"No thank you Don, sometimes coffee keeps me awake at night."
"Me too, may I suggest we retire to the bar, as I really fancy a Cognac, you may have a liqueur if you prefer, I think their Gran Marnier or Cointreau are superb."
"Yes I think I shall have a Grand Marnier, Don, which cognac are you having?"
"Well, I won't go for the best, but I think a Remy Martin will do me!
(**The drinks were served quite quickly**)
"Cheers Elizabeth, let's drink to our holiday."
"Cheers Don, that was a superb dinner, them Crepes Suzettes were delightful, never had them before and the wine really fine, a wonderful choice, I could taste that smoky and plum flavour, and this liqueur is so delicate."
"Yes you are right about the wine, that's why it's called fume' and in the

Crepes Suzettes there was Grand Marnier too with a touch of orange Curacao and flambé with cognac.

"Well, well... Your knowledge in food and wines really amazes me!"

"Well, I must tell you a secret, first few times I entertained some of our customers, I felt somehow, embarrassed, for instance about choosing wine, so I thought there must be a better way to do this, easy really, I went to the library and got some books of catering and the knowhow of the etiquette of dining, that was very interesting to read before I fell asleep....And it thought me to live amongst these toffee chaps....don't laugh, some even thought I came from a high society family.....ha,ha,ha, I tell you that was quite impressive"

"I am speechless Don....... Oh I admire you so much! You are so clever!"

"You are clever too Elizabeth, I think you are extra good at your job, in compare to a few others we have in some other offices, and finally, I think after such a long day we now deserve a few hours of rest."

"Jolly good idea!"

(As they took leave for their own bedroom thanking each other for the lovely evening. Elizabeth had to break the silent atmosphere by saying:)

"Don..... Tonight you have made me the happiest girl in the world, I like you so much!"

"What else can I say? It has been a great pleasure I really did enjoy every minute of it myself, and..... I like you too Elizabeth, it's just the fact that sometimes I cannot find the right words when I am with a beautiful girl like you, however, tomorrow we shall visit some nice places, and for the evening dinner, we shall go to a very special place, don't ask, just wait and see, in the meantime I wish you a very good night **(giving a peck on her cheek, making her blush)** and I will see you around eight am for breakfast!"

"Good night Don, see you in the morning, and thank you again!"

(Don could hardly go back to sleep after that beautiful dinner with Elizabeth, and could not forgive himself for giving her a peck on her cheek. In his mind he kept thinking, am I on holiday with my sister? Why, oh why would he not do or express himself to Elizabeth some true feelings that a beautiful like her would really deserve, he didn't dislike her, on the contrary, he did fancy her quite a bit, but he was afraid to commit himself to do or to say something that he would regret later, he thought; "she is so beautiful and very intelligent, perhaps he could achieve more in life if he would marry her, she's so perfect, as a housewife to a business woman, in the end he felt so confused, and decided to wait for the next day and see what his mind would tell him to do. A quick look at his watch and realized that it was nearly three am, and he thought: "At this rate I'll be awake all night long, I wonder if I am falling in love with that girl...... No.... that cannot be" And so Don finally fell asleep until the telephone rung for the wakeup call that the night before he had asked the reception.)

(Don lied awake for ten minutes or so, thinking again about Elizabeth before getting in the bath...."She so clever that girl, sometimes she amazes me, she knows how behave in a place like this" While the water was running in the bath, Don jumped in as he didn't want to be late. He looked out of the window and glad he was to see a beautiful sunshine, that way he knew exactly what to wear for a hot day, then he thought and thought about the evening visit to the Moulin Rouge...."Yes I must keep that as a surprise, I look forward to see her face as we'll enter that magnificent place. I think I am so lucky to be with a beautiful girl like Elizabeth, perhaps I feel a bit jealous when I see a lot of men staring at her... don't worry Don....that's only normal... **(And so Don kept is mind very active)** some people would give and arm and a leg to be with an attractive girl like her.... she is really gorgeous.... That bath really did me good, I feel ten years younger.... here we go...."

Chapter 6

(Breakfast was served in the main dining room and this time they were both punctual, both smiling and looking forward to their second day in Paris.)

"Good morning Don.... Did you sleep well?"

"I slept alright but I had to read before I went off with the angels, that's what my mother used to tell me as she tucked me in....Yes... she used to say; go on Donald close your eyes and go to sleep with the angels ..... But to tell you the truth, I've never seen any angels at all, they were in my dreams, so I always wondered what they looked like, if they ever exited, naturally!"

"That was lovely Don, your mum must have loved you a lot!"

"Yes she did loved me a lot, maybe because I was the first child, you know the first ones get spoiled tremendously!"

"Yes they do say that the first one gets loved a bit more than the rest! If I ever get married I think I shall have no more than a couple and treated the same... there again who knows what the future will hold, shall we change subject?""

"I think we better.... Today we shall visit Montmartre Elizabeth, that's where all the painters gather, we will certainly enjoy looking at them paintings, we shall have a small lunch in one of the workers bistro, but in the evening we shall have dinner and Champagne........... I might as well tell you... at the famous Moulin Rouge, that's the place where you must drink only Champagne, their shows are superb, so they say! I already asked the reception to book us a table at seven pm, I wanted to keep it a secret but I had to come out with it!"

"Sounds perfect Don, cannot ask for more. I knew you could not keep that secret until tonight, I was really wondering what kind of surprise that was, I can see why, you are so exited and you must have a good reason to be over the moon!

"No special reason really, the fact is that is something that I've always wanted to see the reality of the Moulin Rouge, according to what I read in the newspapers, it is the number one spot in Paris, we both deserve to see and try it. I am sure you'll love it Elizabeth and there are more plenty places to see, we must make the best of it while we here!"

"Oh... no need to tell you how much I look forward to see the wonders of Paris!"

(Elizabeth was over the moon to so many painters in Montmartre)

"You know if I live here I would have my place full of those paintings, I know there many painters in England as well, but the French somehow, the give me some kind of sensation, that I feel great pleasure to look at them!"
"True Elizabeth, I couldn't agree with you more, they are very interesting, and more than anything their colours are really something!"
"So glad to hear your view, perhaps we have the same taste in many things Don, as you seem to agree all the time even in the office!"
"Well... I do agree in many things you do for the simple fact that most of the time I couldn't do them better myself, and of course as I said that before, I couldn't write letters as good as you do, you are my tutor!"
"Don there's no need to exaggerate, I'm sure the day I will leave the company you will soon find a better secretary than me!"
"Nonsense, if you leave the company I shall come with you!"
"Is it a promise or a treat?"
"It's a promise, but if I will leave before you, you must promise that we will see each other just the same!"
"It's a deal Don!"
"As far as I'm concern it's a deal for me too. Thank you darling... shame we can't take back a few painting with us!"
"Never mind Don, I'm sure there'll be another time!"

(After their enjoyable day, they met at six pm in the Hotel foyer, ready to catch a taxi to the Moulin Rouge, which incidentally it was there already)

"Bonsoir Mademoiselle Elizabeth, Moulin Rouge here we come!" **(with a little peck on her cheek)**
"Bonsoir Monsieur Don... See? I have practiced my French too!" **(Blushing.... and very pleased)**
"Please allow me!" **(Opening the door's taxi)**
"Oh you are such a gentleman... thank you Don!"
"Merci... Le Moulin Rouge s'il vous plait **(to the driver)**
"Mais oui monsieur!"
" Here we go darling, I just can't wait to see it!"
"That's what I thought...."

(They arrived at the Moulin Rouge in good time, the driver in the taxi spoke a little English, so they had no linguistic problems, but on entering Don tried his French.)

"Bonsoir Monsieur on il a reserve' un table pour deux, s'il vous plait....Donald et mon nome

"Mais oui Monsieur Donald, suivre' moi, monsieur je parle Anglais aussi!"

"That is perfect then... I think we better speak English....!"

"Goodness me, Don you are doing well.... I am really proud of your French"

"Merci Mademoiselle Elizabeth, but from now, as I said, I shall have to speak my lingo, all this thinking wears me out, anyway not only that, I must admit I have run out of French words, good job this chap speaks English!"

"As you wish Don.... Oh, look at them lovely pictures, the walls are almost full."

"Oh yes, I forgot to tell you; Did you know that this is also the place, where the famous painter Touluse Lautrec spent most of his time in the late nineteen century? Painting elegant and provocative images of the modern art of those times, of course? He was from an aristocratic family, he was also an handicap.... sad really, in saying that, they say he was in love with the famous cancan dancer La Goulue', there's a nice painting of her hanging somewhere, so I read...... he was so talented!"

"Very interesting, I am learning a lot this week Don!"

"Voila monsieur Donald, vôtre table!"

"Merci! Oh, can we have a bottle of champagne please, Dom Perignon, vintage preferably!

"Mais oui Monsieur.... je vous appelle le sommelier!"

"Don what did he say?

"He said he's going to send us the wine waiter...or something like that!"

(Their table wasn't very far from the stage, which gave them a superb view, their dinner was first class, they started with some foie gras, a very special pate' followed with Lobster Thermidor and a choice from the sweet trolley, of course the Dom Perignon Champagne made their meal perfect, not to mention the show which was out of this world, the dancers were unbelievably very good, everything was as Don imagined and of course what he expected.)

(They arrived back at the hotel by taxi at eleven pm. they sat in the bar for a little night cup)

"So you liked the Moulin Rouge Elizabeth, you must admit that is something different than some places in London!"
"Yes Don, I don't think there are no such venues of that kind at all in London, not that I know, anyway!"
"True Elizabeth, but before we say anything else, I think we should have a night cup, what would you like, before you go and see the angels?"
"Ah, ah, ah, You are just hilarious Don.... that really completed my lovely evening, please don't stop, otherwise I will say you are my angel.....Hoops sorry I didn't mean that, I hope you don't get offended, after all you are my boss!"
"Oh.... Elizabeth, don't be silly, you can say whatever you like, your company is certainly outstanding, I would have been so miserable on my own... I envy that lucky fellow, that will swipe you off your feet, but there again, please don't say a word, I don't really want to know your secrets, I rather want to tell you one of my secrets, but before let me order a drink for you.... May I suggest a crème de menthe frappe?"
"That'll be lovely Don...thank you!"
"Okay... and I shall have a nice brandy....Garcon....!"
"Monsieur....."
"Crème de menthe for the lady, and Remy Martin for me....Merci!"
"Good lord these waiters they are very polite, aren't they?"
"Oh yes they are indeed Elizabeth, in a place like this they must conduct themselves properly, people pay quite good money and for this they expect to get a very good service... As I was saying before about this other ambition of mine, it might not be as good as my knowledge in my current job, but please hear me out!"
"Yes I would like to hear about your other ambition...I have no doubts that you'll reveal something extraordinary"
"Well... after what I have experienced and seen, at the Moulin Rouge, London is craving for a place like that, but if I had my way, I wouldn't have a place as expensive as such, and not as big, the bigger the place, more problems it can creates, I would have a place where everyone would be able to afford it and have a good time, without spending a fortune, don't forget we are still going through a world recession, and sometime is better to have an egg today than a chicken tomorrow, in

saying that it's only an idea which I consider it as a dream, maybe it is the cognac that speaks, silly dreams! By the way, we must not forget to pick up the photo we have done at the Moulin Rouge, they said it would be ready in a couple of days, after all we paid for it!"

"Well... you paid for it, just to put things strait... I certainly will remind you Don, I'm really looking forward to see it!"

"I'm really honoured to be in it with you Elizabeth! Oh... By the way, I Put the Moulin Rouge card in the Hotel post box for Mr Willis, he did ask me for it, I'm sure he'll like that"

"Yes.....He'll be really very pleased to see it, I'm sure he'll appreciate them lovely dancers on it....ah, ah, ah, ah, ah!"

"I'm sure he will......ha,ha,ha,ha,!"

"Don.... about that dream of yours.... you are worrying me, I know you and believe me this is a woman intuition, if you decide to make any dream come true, no one can stop you, and I know very well that you will do it!"

"Good Lord, I think you are a mind reader too, but I like your convincing thoughts about me, I don't know if this is the right word but I thank you for it and the reality is; it would be a great challenge, and forgive me that second cognac made me a little tired, we had a long day, and an exciting one too!"

"Yes Don, I feel the same if you don't mind me saying so."

"Usual time for breakfast and tomorrow we shall climb the Tour Eiffel, the Eiffel tower to you and me, and we shall watch almost all the roofs of Paris.....and all the bridges... naturally, and all the lovers going by!"

(And so they both bid goodnight to each other, with the usual peck on her cheek, and yet once again Don did not have the courage to express his feelings with Elizabeth, knowing quite well the way she felt about him, he thought she must have felt disappointed about not declaring his feelings, although she knew exactly that deep down he fancied her, but she could never understand, why....oh....why... he never showed any loving feelings, although he liked her very much, perhaps not as much as she liked him, or maybe he was hiding another secret love in his heart)

Chapter 7

(That fantastic week ended too soon, they certainly did not miss many others important places to visit, the most memorable was of course the Moulin Rouge, and they did collect the photograph to reminding them of their good time in Paris, of course they only had one done and Don gave it to Elizabeth which she safely kept in one of the Paris illustrations book. They also brought back two little presents for Mr Willis, a miniature of the Eiffel Tower and two bottles of a very expensive red Bordeaux vintage wine in a wooden box, which Mr Willis loved tremendously, Don was quite sure that he would be over the moon with such wine. No matter how small the present were, the chairman would really appreciated them)

(They arrived back late at night, Don invited her back to his bungalow for a quick night cup, but Elizabeth declined, she said that she was feeling rather tired, Don was quite surprised, maybe he didn't expect it)

"Are sure you won't stop even for a cup of tea Elizabeth, I hope I didn't offend you by asking you that, at this time of night!"

"How can you say that Don? You can ask me anything you like and I will do it for you, but tonight I feel so tired, I just don't think I'll be able to keep my eyes open for another ten minutes, maybe I had more than one glass of wine on that ferry, which was superb and that fish and chips brought back some old memories from my mum and dad, they loved their fish with a slash of vinegar on the chips, mind you, not accompanied with wine but they used to have a nice cup of tea, to tell you the truth I did enjoy it with a couple of glasses of wine!"

"I'm so glad you enjoyed that, actually I love a good fish and chip now and then, with some vinegar on the chips too, unlike in the restaurant you must have it with tartare sauce... very posh! However, about the night cup I do understand dear, and please accept my apologies, I don't want you to think that I was pushing you!"

"Please Don... don't apologize... I had the most wonderful week in my life!" **(Elizabeth started crying and embraced Don with so much love that he felt touched but somehow embarrassed)**

"Darling.... Please don't cry, I had the most wonderful week with you too, **(At this point he holds her tight and for the first time they kiss passionately)** Oh.. I'm so sorry darling I didn't mean to, it's just that I...

Yes I felt quite sorry for you... Please forgive me.... No.... I don't feel sorry for you, I shouldn't have said that!"

"Oh Don...I love you so much, I just don't know what to say, I wanted to say it in Paris, but I thought it wouldn't have been a lady like to say such word that way, I mean expressing my feelings for you, Although I guess you might not feel the same about me!"

"I know you do darling.... but I feel a bit confused about my feelings. For the past week I just asked myself why couldn't I expressed what I really wanted to say to you...? I really feel confoundedly, and annoyed with myself Elizabeth... anyway I'll see you at the office tomorrow, and let us keep this conversation a secret for the moment, in saying that I am really sorry to see you so tired!"

"Good night Don and thank you for everything, no matter what happen I shall never forget our wonderful week in Paris!"

"Good night Elizabeth, me too, I never felt so relaxed for such a long time, you are just fantastic....and adorable!"

(Once again they embrace, this time with the a little kiss on the cheek)

(Next day Don was back rather early at the office but just before his lunch break he thought to pay a visit to Mr Willis, and take the presents, for sure he would want to know some good news, not only about the holiday, but about the week with Elizabeth, so Doreen his secretary was there)

"Hello Doreen.... is Mr Willis available?"

"Oh hello Don... nice to see you back, I trust you had a pleasant holiday in Paris, and did Elizabeth enjoyed too?"

(Don thought; this is bloody embarrassing, I bet all staff know)

"That was a fantastic week Doreen I wish you were there too!"

"I don't think my husband would allow me for such a holiday, who'd look after the kids then?"

"I think a good French holiday would do you good, instead of going to Margate every summer!"

"We love that Don, they make the best fish and chips with mashie peas in the world, and my hubby wouldn't miss his English Ale, he does drink quite a few pints of that...I tell you!"

"If you say so Doreen... can I go in to see Mr Willis then?

"Of course my dear, I think is expecting you, he already asked me a couple of times if you were in your office!"

(Knock..knock)

"Coming... whoever you are!"

"Good morning Mr Willis... it's only me, I hope I'm not disturbing!"

"Oh... hello...Nice to see you back Donald, I can see that you look a new man... thank you for Moulin Rouge post card, did you enjoy it... Was the hotel alright?"

"Oh... Everything was absolutely out of this world, and so other places, we had a fantastic week, I simply don't know how much we appreciated your kind gesture, Elizabeth was over the moon, she told me she will write you a thank you card!"

"Never mind about that, you both deserved it, tell me Donald anything unusual happened... or any good news? You know what I mean my boy!"

"No... nothing's happened.. you know me Mr Willis, sometimes I am afraid to say something that I shouldn't, and to be quite honest I am not so sure I would make the right decision, anyway, Elizabeth is so nice and we both got on like as we have known each other for years of course, the problem is, I'm not so sure that she would want me, naturally it is quite difficult to make the right decision sometimes, but we never know, time will tell... she really is a fantastic girl, and a good secretary if I may say so!"

"For goodness sake Donald snap out of it, I like that girl.. and she's mad about you... everyone knows that, she's crazy about you, you need a bit of sunshine in your life....Oh... I wish I was younger again, you wouldn't stand a chance"

"I know Mr Willis, I will seriously think about that, I need more time, in the meantime I shall have to go as I have quite a few appointments to sort out, actually the first one is with one of the Directors of the Gulf Company, one of our best supplier!"

"Yes you are right, try to keeping him happy the best you can, he always looks so miserable, bloody people, the more money they make, the more unhappy they are!

"I know that Mr Willis, we must keep them happy them lot...Oh here...that's for you Mr Willis we thought you'll like these they are good Bordeaux vintages and of course a little Eiffel Tower from Elizabeth!"

"Oh what a lovely thought... will you thank her for me please? And as for these two chateau bottles I will surely enjoy them with my favourite sirloin steak, my wife really can cook it the way I like it....it is indeed my favourite wine, I just couldn't go without, it's the only pleasure I've got left in life, if you don't mind me saying so! "

" Yes, that is a very good wine, we had couple of bottles ourselves too in Paris, and talking about our customers, you are so right Mr Willis, they are never satisfy!"

"Make sure you fill up their glasses, of whatever they drink, they make me laugh, they forbid their people to drink alcohol, and they get drunk twenty four seven when they out of their country!"

"Ah, ah, ah, I sincerely hope they keep their prices, at a good level!"

"Okay Donald...Try your best and take it easy...More than anything...... keep smiling!"

"Just leave to me Mr Willis, I shall do my best!"

(Six months went by without any problems and Elizabeth seems to be waiting for Don to make his magic move, although they have been out a couple of times for dinner together to revive that wonderful week in Paris, but the situation so far has been standing still and one morning...)

"Good morning Elizabeth, how are you to day?"

"Good morning Don, I'm very well thank you... and you?"

"Oh... not too bad, when you finishing that letter, can you come into my office please?"

"Don't tell me is another week in Paris...ah, ah, ah, ah!"

(Don is smiling)

"Nothing of the sort Elizabeth!"

(Ten minutes later)

"Please come in Elizabeth and take a seat!"

"Thank you Don... I don't know whether I should look forward to this or not... I only hope it's not too serious!"

"Not really Elizabeth, but before I proceed to say what I'm going to tell you, I would like you to remember that you are the first to know it!"

"Okay let's hear it then... please don't keep me in suspense!"

"Right... Elizabeth I have decided to leave the company, I have been here now for the past sixteen years, and I think a change will do me a lot of good!"

(Elizabeth was speechless for a minute or two)

I hope I haven't shocked you darling!"

"In a way you didn't as I know you are really an entrepreneur, I expected that, and yes, I guess that was the Moulin Rouge... was it?"

"Perhaps it was, and whatever I shall do you will be the first to know!"
"Thank you Don... I do appreciate your sincerity, can I go now as I have so many letters to write?"
"Yes you may go Elizabeth, but what's the rush, I hope I didn't upset you in any ways!"
"No...no... you didn't...but I must go and finish my work, if you don't mind, he's been piling up lately!"
"Okay as you wish Elizabeth.... see you later!"
(An hour later Elizabeth knocks at Don's office door)
"Coming... please coming...,. Oh it's you Elizabeth!"
"Will you please sing these letters, they are important that they should leave with this morning post!"
"Of course my dear **(They look in each other eyes and Don can see that she's been crying)** Why Elizabeth, why oh why? You don't have to upset yourself for what I said!"
"Please Don... don't make me say what you don't really want to hear, but if you must know, yes I am upset, this is the worst news I had to put up with for a long time, you know dam well how much I love you, of course it's not your fault, you haven't done anything to make me feel like that, in a way I wish you did, yes I wish you did when we were in Paris, I wanted you so much, and yet nothing did happened, I really wished you did something at least I would have something to remind me of the good times..... and...."
"Darling, just because I leave, it doesn't mean that we are not going to see each other again, is that what you think?"
"Probably it is, because I know you, when you do something you have no time for anyone!"
"That is not true, I even was thinking that if my new venture is successful I would even ask you to be my partner!"
"Partner in what.... business? No thank you, I just want you to be your partner in another way!"
"Well... this is now a surprise for me, I don't think I am ready for that, but please let's not fall out....Please? **(in that moment Don gets up and embraces her and kiss her passionately for the second time)**
"That's wonderful Don, at least I've got two kisses to reminds me of the good times with my only love! Can I go and finish the rest of the letters now?
"Yes darling.... do I have a choice?"
"Yes you might have... see you later Don!"

Chapter 8

(So after working for sixteen years for "Liquid Gold & Co" Don decides to leave the company. It was quite a shock for Mr Willis but as Don was a shareholder Mr Willis decided to make him a Director of their board, which it meant he would have to sit with the others Directors at the AGM)

"I just don't know what to say Mr Willis, considering I am not working here and yet you nominated me for such position, I am so grateful!"
"Never mind about that Donald, I want you to be on the Board and to keep an eye on the business, if you see anything wrong, you just report it to me, I am the Chairman and the boss, in the meantime just go and do what you like, don't forget that you are still on the payroll, and we need your presence whenever we have important meetings, I suppose that will be a couple of times a year!"
"Thank you Mr Willis, I understand exactly what you mean, and I'm honoured to serve you and the company!"
"Thank you Donald, I will instruct my lawyer to draw up the agreement and make sure you'll sign it. I wish you all the best...Bye, bye!"
"Goodbye Mr Willis and thank you very much!"

(Sadness is all around especially for Elizabeth who she still waiting for Don to propose, but in the end , maybe she's not made for him. The company gave him a great send off, with a big party, a big cheque and many presents from his colleagues. Elizabeth gave him a little packet which he opened when he arrived at his bungalow, inside there was a photo framed they had taken at the Moulin Rouge, with a note written on the back "I will always love you" Elizabeth xx PS: `I had a copy made of it.` This gentle touch present gave Don a few tears of loneliness. Few days later he sent her a letter, thanking her for the photo-framed, and saying he understood her feelings, but he felt somehow not quite ready for married life promising to keep in touch in the future, signed with hugs and kisses.)
(Don was just about ready for his new venture, put his bungalow up for sale, naturally for the moment he kept the three bedroom house, just in case his family wanted to visit him, actually it didn't need to sell neither of them, as he wasn't short for a bob or two, plus he kept all his shares in Liquid Gold making good returns and of course he was still

getting paid by the company for being a Director. So he started to walk around London in search for something he had in mind. After a week he came across an old empty building right in the centre of London, perhaps that was more or less what he had been looking for, looking at its references it turned out to be quite a well know show house in the nineteen twenties, after a good search by a surveyor, it turned out to be okay and exactly what he wanted. The offer was made, and both parties were happy with the price, and an application was made to the local Council for what he had in mind. Naturally it needed completely refurbished, and after summing up the repairs costs and the contents, as the building was completely empty, he was very confident to afford all the expenses. The agent who dealt with Don's future property was twenty years old Bertie Smith and Don was quite impressed about him after he heard his suggestions as a seller, which after all they were very favourable to Don's ideas, Don liked him so much that he offered him a job in his new venture. Bertie accepted with no hesitation.....)

"Welcome to my new business Bertie, if I may call you that, you may call me Don, next we'll have to talk about your wages and I promise you it won't be less than you are earning now, I believe in looking after my staff properly, as I expect them to look after my profits!"
"Thank you Don, I can see you are a gentleman, and I am glad about the job offer, selling properties is never been my choice, not many people buys properties now days, and considering the low wages we get plus commission it's not enough to have a decent living when you are married!"
"Any children yet?
"Not really, we only have been married for two years."
"AH... you are still on honeymoon my dear boy!"
"So everyone says.... by the way Don, I think I shall have to give two weeks notice to my boss, is that alright?
"Of course Bertie, you must do things properly, that's how you earn respect. anyway you have got my phone number, when you finish with your firm or anytime before just give us a ring and we shall put something on paper, kind of contract, in the meantime I shall work on some more drawings and a good name!"
"As we are near Piccadilly Don, why not call it **"The Piccadilly Tavern"**
"I think I like that, and I am sure it will be fine with a nineteen twenty style decor, with a little stage, some dancing girls and the old Joanna,

and selling real true good English Ale and good food!"
"I think I like that Don, a place really that anyone can afford to patronise, selling from Champagne to cider or beer!"
"Bertie you've got good ideas, you seem to read my mind."
"Nice to have met you Don, I shall look forward to be at your service. I'm sure we will do great things, I can see your project already in action. Can't wait to tell my Mrs. for sure she'll will be happy."
"What's the name of your Mrs, if I may ask?"
"Rosie...... and she's beautiful......."
"Beautiful like a rose you mean! It's a beautiful name indeed!"
"Just like a rose Don!"
"Okay Bertie, go back to your office and tell them the property is mine, I will instruct my solicitor today as I want the deal moving as fast as it can, and you, gently give them your notice, but not a word where you are going or about my project yet, in the meantime good luck to both of us! See you soon."
"Trust me Don, I just can't wait for this new venture to start, I've got a few more ideas how to get the place going you'll see!"
"Can't wait, to hear the rest, look after yourself and see you soon!"

(With a good old hand shake, they both say goodbye to each other. Don knows exactly that he's not alone, as he believes that Bertie is the man he really needs for his new venture.)

(Few weeks later work started and Bertie was there every day, to see that the workers were doing their job properly and assisting Don organizing whatever material was needed, to make the show house live and better, more like a land mark for the capital of England.)

(The Piccadilly Tavern is almost completed. The decor is very tastefully, nineteen twenty style as planned. On the large double doors entrance there's a sign; **"WE LIKE YOU FOR WHAT YOU ARE WHETHER YOU LIVE NEAR OR FAR"** There's a little stage on the left end corner with its mahogany old Joanna and golden stool. Bertie managed to introduced to Don a piano player whom he has known for a long time called Charlie, in fact Bertie used to sing with him a few years back, quite an expert with his musical knowledge. The stage has red, blue and gold drapes hanging either sides, giving ease in and out to the dancing girls, and lots of beautiful roaring twenties pictures around the walls premises. The long counter bar is facing the entrance with a grand display of bottles on their shelves, and two latest fashion cash registers. There are three large wooden barrels under the shelves for the choice of the local classic Ale, and one small barrel on the counter for the old vintage Port, and not to forget the old beer pumps. Two massive mirrors on the back walls' counter displaying the sign; **"Welcome and keep smiling"** And two beautiful flowers vases on each end of the counter. The lounge is surrounded with many little round tables with their golden chairs with red seats, and the six large windows facing the long Regent street displaying the menu and drinks prices, everything seems to be designed almost to perfection, for a perfect place of entertainment. The opening date is set, most of the staff is trained, but before opening the doors, Don wants to make sure and trains is employees once more just to be certain they do as he thinks best of how the place should be run. On the last day he makes his final checks with his head barman Bertie;)

"We've got to have everything almost to perfection Bertie!"
"Couldn't agree with you more Don! Incidentally, I had to employ another kitchen porter as the previous one was indispose!"
"Jolly good Bertie, you do what you think best!"

(At last the opening night is here, Ivy the waitress is at the door offering to every customer coming in a glass of Madeira and some miniatures pork pies and spiced pork scratching to wet the appetite. The dancers open the evening with a new Charleston song simply called "Love and Champagne" especially written by Charlie and Bertie, this is sung by the five girls and the main singer Lisa. Don welcomes everyone with a smile, except he's a bit disappointed that Elizabeth his ex secretary hasn't turned up, he did send her an invitation, she replied that she would try her best to come.)

"Hi Bertie, my ex secretary hasn't turned up, so far, I am quite disappointed and very sad, I was counting on her to be here, perhaps you'd be so kind to remind me tomorrow to give her a call, and see what happened, shame really, I was really looking forward to see her, she was ever so good to me, in a funny way I do feel sorry to have disappointed her, about her feelings towards me!"

"Well Don.... For what I know she was not only good to you, but quite fond of you, maybe if she had come, she would felt out of place, seeing you very busy with other customers, she wouldn't have known anybody else but you, and you..... certainly wouldn't had had time to keep her company, so I think it's better like that!"

"Maybe you are right Bertie, I like her very much, but not the way she likes me!"

"You must have someone else in mind then Don.....eh?"

"Oh, no one at the moment, I can assure you, I am too busy getting this place going, if you see what I mean...."

"I know exactly what you mean Don!" Oh, I think they need some help behind the bar......

"Just leave that to me Bertie I'd like try and mix with the workers behind the bar, lot off customers seem to be ordering their food too, and I can see they need a hand taking orders."

"I will start to take some orders myself and I think I better call Ivy and tell her to start collecting dirty glasses, goodness me, we don't seem to have enough table to accommodate everyone!"

"Well... we'll have to think of getting some more table and chairs, we have enough room anyway!"

"We can order them tomorrow Don!"

"Right you are Bertie, and also we must order some more menus!"

(The menu is quite simple really. Quite a lot of choice of pork pies, lots of cold meats, freshly fried fish and chips and many other snacks. It looks like all the plates are coming back clean. The end of the first evening seemed to have come to conclusion quite fast, everyone's gone, the staff are tidying up the place for the next morning's cleaners. Before dispensing the staff, Don wishes to say a few words;)

"Ladies and gentlemen I thank you for your great effort and excellent work that you've carried out tonight, I am proud of you all and I hope we will make this place very successful in the coming days, naturally without you I won't be able to achieve this, so, I say thank you once again and God bless you all...... Goodnight....."

Chapter 9

(Nearly one year went by and the Tavern was acquiring more fame than he wished for, naturally the local press seemed to have given more notoriety, Don didn't need any advertising as he even had the pleasant visit from the LMR the well known network London Mercury Radio station whom they recorded a couple of songs and interviewed Lisa the girls and Charlie, naturally they were over the moon and certainly this contributed a lot as an incentive for the business, in other words the Tavern became the talk of the town. As usual before opening its doors, Don makes the final checks.)

"You know Don, each evening when we open the doors I can see in your eyes the pleasure you get to own such a wonderful place!"
"You are right Bertie, I worked very hard to get where I am, from a simple soldier, to a kitchen porter, a decent accountant with a simple Diploma and here I am to run this wonderful place with a special licence, and please may i say there I'm still a director of my old firm!"
"What a lovely story, you could write a book Don."
"I might do that one day.....Yes, I could do that during my retirement days, that is, if I will get to old age and with all my faculties working properly.... I mean my brains!"
"You'll be alright... you'll be always active as ever. Hope you will mention my name Don!"
"Rest assure Bertie, you'll be one of the first, and let me thank you again. I wouldn't have bought this place if you had not been there at the right time, I could see then in you, your capabilities and full of good ideas as a selling property agent, your suggestions were first class!"
"Well, I think you bought it because you liked it, I did sell a lot of properties for that firm, and made a lot of good suggestions to buyers I've got to say, that they didn't treat their staff like you do, for a start they never gave me the right commission as promised, which I duly deserved, or even a bonus, never the less it was a job, and grateful to have one, because if I complained I'm sure they would have turned around and say; if don't like it, that's the door. However, I say thank you for your kind words of appreciation."
"Don't mention it Bertie, I'm only saying what's to be said, in saying that I'd like to say again a special thank you for your introduction of our wonderful singer Lisa. She's the number one of the Tavern now, and

number one amongst the music publishers of the tin pan alley, they keep bringing new songs here for her to sing, and Charlie do his best to fit some in, this is why our golden girl is getting quite well known, although she is not fully recognised as yet, but one day very soon I guess she will achieve it in good time, and that thanks to you Bertie!"

"Glad to hear that Don, it's that I've known her boy-friend Joe for a long time, we used to gig together and of course, one thing to another, found out that she could sing, better than me and Joe!"

"And very good too Bertie, glad we named her the golden voice, in saying that I am also glad that we have Lucy, she's not only a good dancer, but she can also sing, in fact she took Lisa's place a few tomes, when Lisa took a few days off, and people liked her too!"

"Indeed Bertie, Lucy deserve a bit of glory too."

"And she's good looking too, if I may say so!"

"Now, now Bertie... you keep your eyes off Lucy, You've got your wife Rosie and she's beautiful too, if you don't mind me saying so... pity she can't dance otherwise I would ask her to be on that stage

"I don't think I would let her Don!"

"Hello, hello... you are not jealous, are you Bertie?

"Me jealous...? Naaah....not really!

"Anyway Bertie, we are going to have a very busy evening tonight, due to that great show at the Ambassadors Theatre, so let us make sure there won't be any slip up!"

"One last thing Don, did you ever call Elizabeth, your ex secretary?"

Oh, I certainly did, she said she did not feel very well that day, so I've invited her to come and see me anytime she wish, I hope she will!"

"She won't come Don, unless you can give her a date!"

"I thought of that Bertie but....."

"There's no buts, you must call her again, after all I'd like to see what she looks like!"

"Well, I can tell you she is very, very pretty, she has good manners, very intelligent, she dresses well, she like good food, she likes intelligent people, but somehow she's not my type!"

"I can see you couldn't have given me a clearer picture of her!"

"Yes.... that what she is, I don't have to lie, in spite of all, she done a lot for me, I must be honest with you Bertie, when we went to Paris, I was very tempted, I shouldn't say this to you, but I knew she was mine, we had a couple of cuddles and a few kisses but that' as far as we went. I could see in her smile, in her eyes that she loved me one hundred per cent, believe me, but I didn't want to hurt her feelings, knowing she would do anything for me, dam it... sometimes I miss her!"

"Yes....I believe you miss her alright.... I do understand now.... Oh, I forgot to tell you Don, I bought today some British little flags to put around the place for tomorrow's Tavern first Anniversary, they will look just fine... after all this is Britain and we got to keep our name up"

"Right oh, Bertie, let us show everyone that we are proud of good old England. bye the way, I was thinking about Lisa again, I hope she doesn't get any ideas of joining some music hall company, you know damn well Bertie she's a great asset here in the Tavern, let's face it her voice, her personality is out of this world, we couldn't be any luckier, good Lord I keep repeating myself!"

"No.... You are not repeating yourself Don, Lisa is very good, I don't think Joe her boy-friend realizes how good she is, mind you they have known each other since school days, perhaps that's where she learned how to sing, Joe is a couple of years older than her, fact is they mad about each other, they have been living together for a few year now, I suppose they find it cheaper, instead renting two places, some people find this set up very unusual, as they are not married, and yet there's no sign of the eternal ring, I expect it won't be long!"

"I suppose it doesn't mean much living together Bertie, unless you wish to respect religion, Where I come from they call it 'living in sin' ah, ah, ah, ah!"

"That's quite funny Don, let's take it with a pinch of salt, I don't think Joe is very a religious man, but he's certainly a good Christian, anyway, let's hope we can keep her for a long time! What a wonderful set up we have with Lucy as the understudy you might say!"

"I understand that Lisa was adopted right, and yet I asked her to bring her parents so to speak, whom I would like to meet and yet....."

"Don't think she's ashamed of them, the fact is that this is not their kind environment, I met them a couple of times, they are very pleasant, but a little bit old fashioned I'd say!"

"And what happened to her real parents?

"Unfortunately they died in a car accident somewhere in Liverpool, but she has accepted it now!"

"Sad really, I had to live my parents too, when I was in my twenties, but my situation was different, I had to, where I come from there was no work at all, so I had to emigrate, sort of, naturally the great war was to blame for that!"

"So I heard Don, you must have gone through some very hard times!"
"Oh well... that was the past, I think we'll have a great future in front of us, you've got to be positive in life!"
"Very good words of wisdom, thank you Don!"
"Time is getting on, let us open the doors, get some more ice in the buckets Bertie, oh... we need some more bottles of Ale!"

(Don walks over to Charlie and the dancers)

"Hello young Charlie... are you ready... and full of stamina as usual?"
"Never been so fit Don, look at my little darlings, they are smiling and looking forward to show their new dance routine we coordinated this afternoon...."
"Glad to hear that Charlie, and one of this days you must tell me how could you write that wonderful Charleston.... so catchy!"
"Yes, love and Champagne, very easy song, but let us not forget the cooperation of Bertie, he wrote most of the lyrics, and in actual fact it was his idea of the title!"
"Hawh...... Bertie never stops to amaze me, he's a very intelligent fellow...... I think I better open the doors Charlie, I can see quite a few people waiting outside!"

(Don opens the doors and Charlie starts counting... one..two..three... four... off we go girls......

Lyrics (Chorus)

Love and champagne/ It's our special hobby/ We drink so much/ That it makes us wobbly!
Too much Champagne/Make us feel so dizzy/ Oh, it's such fun/ Drives us sexy crazy!
Lisa; I dream up castles in the air/ with an handsome blue-eyed king!
He kisses me with that gentle touch/ That I love.. yes, far too much!

Chorus

Love and Champagne/ This is all we can do/ Let us enjoy/ This is from us to you!
Let us enjoy/ This is from us to you/ Let us enjoy/ This is from us to you......!

"Wonderful, well done girls, I really like that new dance, no need for me to tell you anything else, those clapping are enough to confirm your professionalism, what a ovation!"

"Yes Don, they are pretty good our girls!"
"Many thanks Charlie!"

(Don is very pleased to see his customers enjoying the good show, so pleased that he asks Bertie to take a bottle of bubbly to the girls......)

"And Bertie make sure you tell them that it was left in wood last night by one of their admires, I don't really want to get any idea that it's from me, and leave it in the ice bucket on their table, that way we'll show our customers that we sell the expensive drinks too, tell them also, to make it last, the evening is long!"
"I see what you mean Don, you just want to give them more incentive about their performance, and your profits too!"
"Bertieeee... I thought you never guessed it, that's what I call show business!"
"There you are girls, this was left in the wood last night from the compliments of a very well off admirer... please don' ask who he was... ah,ah,ah, I presume he has a lot of money to please you all!"
"Yes, we could do with someone with a lot of money. However, Many thanks Bertie, who ever paid for it we will drink it to his good heath!"
"Don't mention it Lucy, and don't forget to go easy on it, the boss said the evening is long, in other words, we don't want to see you falling asleep on the stage.... only joking'...."
"Even when he jokes he's adorable that Bertie, They say his wife Rosie is very jealous of him..."
"That's right Jane, she's very jealous she does keep on eye on him all the time, so, you better keep your eyes off of him then..."
"You can shout Lucy I see you often enough smiling at him...and.."
"Come on you two, he's a married man, you should not even think of it... young married men snatchers!"
"That's fine for you Lisa, you've got a man!"
"Sorry Jane, I only thought you deserve a single fellow!"
"You mean someone like Bertie..."
"Of course she means that Lucy!"
"See.... Jane? Lucy's right, never get involved with a married man, they mean troubles, I'm surprise of Bertie, he never argue with his Rosie.
"Yes you are right girls, I couldn't avoid hearing your comments!"
"I wouldn't take any notice Don, they are only talking about their fantasies!"

"Oh, is that so girls? Never mind, you are young and all beautiful and you have the rights to talk about your feelings, and once again I just love your new dance routine, so, keep on doing your best! By the way Lisa, you haven't sung that beautiful swing called; "First love is so beautiful" I really missed that, you do it so well, with that jazzy touch, that really reminded me of my younger days!"
"Right you are Don, that will be no problems, I am sure Charlie will oblige, can you pass me the score Charlie, I'm not so sure about the lyrics;
"There you are Lisa, is on page forty three One and one , two, and three..and...."
(In the meantime Bertie was in his office and the phone rang ....)
"Hello... can I help you?"
"Oh hello.... my name is Elizabeth Campbell, I am a friend of Don... Who am I speaking to?"
"You are speaking to Bertie, Bertie Smith, I am his head barman and manager. What can I do for you Miss Campbell?"
"Well... I don't know whether Don mentioned my name to you, but I was wondering to pay him a visit in the near future, is he usually there?"
"Yes he did mention your name a couple of times, he thinks very highly of you. He's here all the time, the man's never stop working, shall I give him a message?"
"Yes, you are right he never stop working, he only finds time for that, no don't give him a message, as I don't know when I can come!"
"Look Miss Campbell, tomorrow it's our first anniversary, I'm sure he would be delighted to see you, why don't you surprise him?"
"Well... I don't really know if I can make it, by the way, you can call me Elizabeth if you wish!"
"Thank you Elizabeth, look...I won't tell him that you phoned, just make him happy and please come and see us tomorrow...I'm sure he'll appreciate that!"
"As a matter of fact I'm going to see a show in the west end tomorrow evening with a friend, I might pop in after the show!"
"That is wonderful Elizabeth, I shall look forward to meet you then!"
"Me too Bertie....Goodbye!"
"Bye, bye Elizabeth!"

(Bertie goes back to the Tavern, as Lisa sings Don's favourite song)

Chapter 10

(Lisa starts singing "(First love is so beautiful)

"First love is so beautiful/It's free and so joyful/It's like vintage champagne/Because is rear and so fine----- First love is fantastic/It is full of magic/It is without real price/It is like true paradise!
It's always there when we feel sad/One single thought and we feel glad/So reassuring, so understanding and everlasting.
First love is so beautiful/It is so delightful/It is like golden sunshine/That's why first love is divine."

(While she sings the song a very distinguish couple comes in and stop right in front of the stage listening until Lisa finishes.)

"Good gracious Louise, she really sung that song with so much feeling and a good foxy rhythm, look at the crowd my dear, they are berserk... clapping, not even in that show we saw, they clapped like that!"
"You are so right Bob, what a beautiful voice!
"Go and seat in that corner darling, I will go to the bar to order a bottle of Champagne!
(Bob approaches the bar)
"Good evening my good man, may we have a bottle of your best Champagne, if you please? we shall be seating over in that corner table!" **(pointing at the lady already there)**
"Yes sir, that'll be no problems!" **(meanwhile Don was monitoring the situation)**
"What a charming couple and what an elegant lady... perhaps you ought to let me serve them.. go on Bertie, be a good chap!"
"It's my pleasure Don, I get the champagne!"
"Oh, many thanks Bertie...... **(few minutes later)**
"Here's the Champagne Don, glasses and a few nibbles are already on the table!"
(Don takes the champagne to the couple)
"Good evening to you and welcome to the Piccadilly Tavern,**(Opening the bottle and pouring a little in the gentleman's glass)** I guess this is your first visit to our Tavern!"
"(Bob) "Yes it is, I presume you are the landlord!
"Yes I am, is there anything else you require? My name is Don, and the

chap with the red bow tie is my head barman and manager, should you need anything else, please do not hesitate to ask, and hope you'll enjoy the champagne too!"

"Yes thank you Don, the champagne is excellent, right temperature I'd say, my compliments!" (**Bop replied)**

(Louise stops Don on his walks looking at him in his eyes)

"Thank you Don I am quite sure we will enjoy it! Let us hope as much as that delightful show we saw at the Ambassador Theatre!"

"Yes I did hear it's achieving a remarkable success, in fact I read the reviews this morning, sounds like they got good voices in it too madam!"

"Well, it looks like you are not short of a good voice in here too, we heard that young lady singing as we came in, must say; she's quite astonishing, and your customers seem to like her a lot!"

"Oh, Lisa... yes Lisa she's our golden voice, the Tavern was the very first place she ever sung as a professional, and I suppose we are very lucky to have her really.... she's a real treasure"

"Yes... I do agree with you, you are indeed very lucky to have her, I am sure one day she will be discovered by a professional music scout... well, in saying that an introduction wouldn't go amiss, my name is Louise and my companion and chauffeur is Robert, Bob to his friends, naturally!"

"Delighted to meet you both, and my name as you know already, but my full name is, Donald, Donald O'Reilly, and please, as I said before, please call me Don, I really do prefer that!"

"Excuse me Don, I don't mean to be inquisitive, but your name and accent sounds very familiar to me!"

"Ooooh, **(smiling)** my dear lady, from the land I come from there are many Dons with an accent like mine, and.....you only have to hear my surname... that will tell you a lot.... further more...."

"Sorry to interrupt you, that might be true Don, but if I may ask; Did you ever lodge in St. Peter road, in the Paddington's district?"

"Of course I did.... in that corner shop, many years ago, how can I forget my very first digs?"

"In that case I am that little girl that you used to call 'Poppet' grown older by over twenty five years!"

(Hearing that, Don's face seemed to change colour, he put his hands on the chair in front of him starting his first words seemingly like he was stuttering...)

"Po....po....pet? I am speechless.... please may I sit down, Mary Louise?"
"But before you sit down Don I will get up..."
(Mary Louise gets up and her and Don have a friendly embrace)
"Of course Don, and, I am so glad that you remember my full name, yes I am Mary Louise Ryan, I didn't have to shock you in that manner, fancy seeing you here? I guess this is only a rear but a wonderful coincidence, please ask your barman to bring another glass, looks like you need a drink, go on don't hesitate... sit down!"
"Well, well... this is a surprise (**putting his hand on his chest)** and a wonderful one too, just fit for the Tavern first anniversary, which is tomorrow, I'd say.... Oh, Louise it seems yesterday I left your parents house, and here we are as if time doesn't exists anymore, this has come so quick, so unbelievably quick, we must call this more than a celebration, you brought back some memories, good lord. you are as pretty as when you were seventeen! Nice to meet you too Bob, **(and looking at Louise)** I cannot believe! Is this really happening? Such a long time without a word either way, naturally on my side there's always been a good reason, my job and my brains kept me chained up, so to speak, **(Bertie comes along with another glass)** Thank you, oh, by the way Bertie, may we have another bottle please? The same one!"
"Yes of course Don, will you be needing clean glasses?"
"No need for that Bertie, since we are drinking the same champagne!"
" I won't be log Don, I'll take the ice bucket so can refill it with some more ice!"
"Thank you! Lovely fellow that Bertie, I'd be lost without him, well... (**holding up his glass to his old friend and Bob)** here's to both of you my good friends, let us drink to the past, but most of all the present, al let us hope for a brighter future, cheers... cheers... cheers!"
Back at the bar Berties' getting ready the bottle and have a little chat with Ivy.
"My goodness, I simply don't know.... what's happening to him, looks as though he has seen a ghost, for a minute I saw him looking into space with his eyes closed, and open them in disbelieve, I've got a feeling that he has a connection with them two, I was worried for a minute!"
"Nothing unusual Bertie, that's typical, especially from old bachelors, mind you that goes for young bachelors too, take your brother Peter for instance, if he was married he wouldn't have the time to put his nose into other's people affairs, no wonder they call him; Nosey Pete!"
"Now.. now then behave yourself Ivy, Don is not that old, okay he might be a bachelor, but definitely not an old man, and don't forget he's got

something to be excited about, being the first anniversary of his Tavern tomorrow. As for my brother, yes, he's a bit of a nosey bugger, I shall have a word with him, I can assure you!"

"Please don't tell him I said so, he might get offended, after all he's a nice fellow.... sometimes!"

"Don't worry Ivy, I won't!" **(Bertie takes the bottle to Don's table)**

"There you are Don, it's nice and chilled, shall I open it?"

"Many thanks Bertie, no, I will open it myself, you've got enough to do over there, just look at them Bob, they are fighting their way who gets served first!"

"That is good business Don....."

"Yes Bob it is! Here's to you both once again, let us drink to this memorable surprise!"

"Yes Don let us drink to your wonderful place, better still to your first anniversary, though it's not until tomorrow, never the less, we are so pleased for you!"

"Thank you Louise, good health to you both, I sincerely hope you have a happy life, as for myself I am quite happy too, except now and then I feel there's something missing!"

"I wouldn't worry about anything else Don, as they say; life begins at forty!"

" Thank God for that, but I am not forty yet! Many thanks Bob, words of wisdom, which I gladly accept..... you know Bob, I was just over twenty when I arrived from Ireland, with just a few pennies in my pocket, got a job in a hotel as a kitchen porter, luckily I found lodgings at Louise parents house, as we know they run a corner shop, lovely people they were, especially Louise mum. Must admit they were extremely good to me, they almost treated me like one of the family, but I soon realize that kitchen pottering wasn't for me, so I had to find a better job, of course long before I studied accountancy but because of the military service in Ireland I could never finish my course but I managed to completed in London, between pots and pans, so to speak, so I gained a diploma which gave me the chance to find a job as a trainee accountant, it was with a big company just outside London, my new boss, liked me so much that I was soon promoted, up and up... for in the end I was one the top directors and a shareholder of the company, of course I am still one of the board as when I left the chairman insisted that I remained a Director so I have to attend board meetings now and then, money was good but a very stressing job, so I felt I needed a sort of a change... And yes I came across this lovely building and bought it ... Awh... I always wanted to own something like this!"

"Well done Don.... this is what I call entrepreneurship, I am so pleased for you, goodness me it's unbelievable!"

"Many thanks Bob I really appreciate your compliment, especially coming from a worker like yourself, it's not an easy job to be a chauffeur, long hours and always prompt to open the doors to your employers.... I hope they treat you well!"

"Yes they do treat me well, I have been working for them many years, and I do get quite good perks, like going out to a theatre, he does treat us to the expenses, and he gives me some time off now and then, especially if they go abroad on holiday I have time off with pay!"

"Blamey, your boss must be extra generous.....So glad to hear that..."

"Yes he does treat us very well, I suppose we are sort part of their family!"

"That shows you Louise that if you are good to your employer, he's good to you too, and I am sure you are a loyal worker too Bob, otherwise he wouldn't treat you like that!"

"I think I am Don, I try to do my best!"

"As for me, I was treated well too, I still got a property in Dagenham, thinking that if this venture would fail I would have somewhere to go, a roof over my head it's very important at my age, but luckily I've got two more floors upstairs which have been refurbished and recently completed, I'd say, I could put two families in them, if I wish to!"

"Quite remarkable really, I guess you'll be selling the other house soon."

"I'm seriously thinking Bob, but it's not a worry, at the moment I've got a good neighbour keeping an eye on it, she' a young widow called Jackie, lovely she is, she won't take any money for it, but I won't have it! Then of course I still have a brother and sister with their families visiting me now and then so they'll have somewhere to stay, in any case there's plenty room here if they ever come!"

Oh, I see, maybe the widow, I mean Jackie she fancies you."

"Oh, nothing like that Louise, to be honest I never gave it a thought!"

"Well Don... you are still young and handsome, I don't think that no woman would refuse you a marriage proposition?"

"Maybe I've been too busy counting my money...ha,ha,ha,ha.. only a joke!"

"Nice joke, but money doesn't make you happy Don!"

"But it comes handy sometimes. Anyway, how's your parents Louise?"

"Sadly my parents are no longer with us, it's a long story!"
"Oh I am sorry to hear that Louise. Did you ever completed you studies, Oh.. I do remember that college, in South Kensington, was it?"
"Yes it was, and I did complete my studies, but in the end I've chosen to work for Lord Simpson as a Housekeeper and private secretary, they are a wonderful family, of course I enjoy more than being a lawyer. So here we have Bob who ferries around the Simpsons and me!"
"I am delighted to hear that you are so happy with your life Louise!"
"Yes I am, I cannot complain Don, and equally, I am so happy to see you have done so well with yourself!"
"True... and compliments accepted, so let have a toast to this happy revival again.. and tell me more!"

Chapter 11

(Nosey Pete, Bertie's brother has been watching closely from the opposite table from where the girls are seating and tells his brother that it's not fair that the dancers should get free champagne.)

"I think I should have a free drink too brother now and then, after all I am a good regular customer, and I feel almost part of the family, plus I think I spend quite a bit of dosh in this place!"
"Yes you are quite right dear bruv, but you are not part of the staff, are you? Therefore if you want a drink, put your hand in your pocket!"
"Tch... typical; family love, (**walks over to the girls)** HI girls... pop around just to congratulate Lisa for that swing she sung, blooming marvellous, really Lisa you can be certain that we consider you part of our clan!"
"That's very generous of you Peter, I didn't know you run a clan....!"
"Didn't mean only you, Lucy too can be part of the family, we are a family... are we not?"
"Count me out Pete!"
"Come on Lucy, why do you have to be so difficult, and I wish you call me Peter like Lisa does!"
"Count yourself lucky I don't call you Nosey, which is more appropriate for a chap like you!"
"I just don't know what's the matter with you people. On the market this morning I couldn't even look at Joe, that he snapped my head off!"
"Oh yes? Was he in a very bad mood then Peter?"
"You telling me Lisa, never seen him so grumpy!"
"I keep telling him that he works too hard, he should take it easy!"
"He was moaning mostly about you Lisa, he was saying you are too nice to the customers and I overheard him saying that you don't treat him fairly..... and....and... a few other things, he's not jealous by any chance, is he? The way he behaves I think he is!"
"There he goes again Lisa, always stirring up troubles!"
"Let him say what he wants Lucy, it won't get him very far. I know for a fact that I haven't done or do nothing wrong, plus I can tell you that I look after him properly!"
"Okay, okay Lisa I am sorry, don't upset yourself, I was only saying what I heard...... You know how petty they are those market sellers"
(In that precise moment Joe walks in)

"Oh Yes? I just had enough of you Nosey, you must have said some of your lies again, one of these days you are going to regret every word you said!"
"Just leave him alone Joe, he doesn't know what he says!"
"Oh yes he knows alright what he says!"
"I bet you had a hard day!"
"You can say that again queeny, what with him behind my back, and... now here with you, I feel like I'm going barmy!"
"Come on mate cheer up.... let's have a drink!"
"No thank you, I've had enough of you all day as it is!"
"I'll tell you what I'll do Joe, I shall do one of my impromptu on the stage, just to cheer you up and show you my hidden talent."
"Your talent..... tch.... Which talent.... Don't make me laugh Nosey, your talent is your gossiping about other people's problems, and nothing else!"
"Go on Peter let us see what you can do!"
"Thank you Lisa...... I knew you were on my side. Hi Charlie.. do you still have that song I gave you last week, which I wrote with my brother?"
"Hold on Peter....ehm.. yes here we are, `I like to make a fool of you` Do you want to sing it?"
"Yes please... make a bit faster in the instrumental bit, as I want to do a bit of tap dancing...That's it Charlie, let me borrow that stick behind the door... I'm ready...off we go......

(Nosey Pete sings)

"I like to make a fool of you,/I get that pleasure, yes I do!/It makes me feel so big a strong,/Alright my friends, could I be wrong?/No one can beat my classic style,/I always get that friendly smile,/From girls I know there's no end,/Sometimes they drive me round the bend!?
But when I see a girl like you,/I don't know really what to do,/I can be yours at any time,/Please tell me when you'll be mine!
If I do make a fool of you,/It's just a phase I'm going through,/Please don't look down just look above,/Be nice to me and be my love../Be nice to me a be my love,/Be nice to me and be my love!"

(Sounds like Peter's done a good performance, according to the punters, cheers and applauds and from the girls too and with a few smiles, probably he didn't expected that much.)

"Good old Pete.. See that girls? After all he can do something useful!"

"Yes...... I can see that you did enjoy his jolly performance Lucy, your eyes were on him all the time, am I seeing a soft spot? Please say yes....And I will forget what you said about him in the past!"
"Of course not Jane.... you must be kidding, I was just checking his timing, yes, he did keep his time alright with the music, and to be quite honest I'm not really interested in men at the moment, especially with him! Got too much on my mind!"
"You've got a point there Lucy, but Peter wouldn't be a bad acquisition, if you know what I mean!"
"Not really Lisa... I don't think I would waste my time with him!"
"I'm sorry to hear that Lucy... he's not all that bad, he might talk too much now and then..."
"You can say that again girls!"
"Don't take any notice of what people say Peter!"
"Did I hear my name mentioned again Lisa?"
"No Peter we were just talking about Charlie's playing."
"I wasn't talking to you Lucy........Anyway, I just don't know how you can put up with this lot Charlie."
"Oh come on Peter they are not a bad bunch!"
"Goodness me you are easy going, no wonder you've been going out with the same girl for five years!"
"There's a reason for that Peter, we just can't afford to get married at the moment, but at least we love each other and we don't keep fighting like you do!"
"It's not my fault, it's them girls..... they keep tormenting me!"
"Oh, I'm sorry sir, were you talking about us then?"
"And if I was..... what's it got to do with you Lucy?"
"Go on Pete, say what you want to say and vanish...."
"Okay, okay Lucy, there's no need to be nasty...have I said something to annoy you?"
"Don't worry Peter, she's only doing that just to confuse you!"
"Okay Jane, I think you are over doing this, how many times do I have to tell you.....you can have him any times..... in fact you'll do me a favour."
"Oh, that is generous of you Lucy, now you are deciding which girl I should have...."
"I didn't mean that, it's all Jane's fault, she keeps on saying that I fancy you....Let me tell you that I don't and that's final!"!"
"Well, let me tell you that I don't fancy you.... that's a start.......I'm a bit thirsty, I'd better get a drink!"

(Peter walks away towards the bar)
"What a cheek... it's all your fault Jane."
"No harm done Lucy... don't take it seriously, he's only trying to wind you up! He likes you really, any blind could see that!"
"Well....I must say, Peter's performance was quite good, in actual fact he should have a little spot of his own each evening, perhaps it would be nice If I mention it to Don, just a suggestion, I would say! What do you think Joe?"
"There you go again, another of your sparkling ideas queeny, you seem to be more interested in other people's life instead of my own. Here I am telling you that I work all day long, and when I come home the place looks like a pigsty..... and...I really want a bit of peace."
"Come on Joe, I think you are exaggerating, don't forget that most days I have to come here to practice my songs and dance routine with Charlie, that's my commitment to my job!"
"Oh yes? Surely you can find time to your chores before that!"
"You must be blind, I do my chores every day, I love you Joe, and...and... I am not neglecting my house work or you, I really don't!"
"Love me? That's a joke, with all the smiling and chatting you do with them lot....
"Them lot pays my wages, don't you ever forget it Joe!"
"You don't seem to understand, do you? I am telling you that you are neglecting me, and you are reminding me of those few pennies that you earn, don't make laugh MY DEAR....those few pennies don't even pay for the coal we burn!"

(Their hotly argument attracted Don, who feels rather embarrassed and uncomfortable for his friends, he calls Bertie and tells him to go and calm them down.)
"Bertie do me a favour, just go and tell them; if they have problems they can sorted out in their own place, and not in here....and please don't be nasty, say it with a smile!"
"I'll do my best Don, leave it to me, after all they are good friends of mine I'm sure they'll listen." **(Off he goes)**

"So sorry about that Louise, quite an unusual commotion, really it never happened before, whatever problems I don't think Lisa deserves it. She's so nice and so much in love with Joe, I don't know what to think or do... I really don't want to lose her!"

"I do understand how you feel Don, so they are in love, eh? She's such a lovely girl, and so talented. Is she from around here?"
"All I know is she come from Suffolk Louise, and I know she was adopted as a young baby, after losing her parents in an accident in Liverpool, Joe has known her since her school days!"
"Have you met her adopted parents then?"
"No they've never been here, perhaps it's not their kind of environment, although I offered Lisa to bring them now and then, as I thought they would be pleased to hear her sing, and I would pleased to meet them too, I find that very odd!"
"Quite an interesting story..... Don we must call it a day, it's almost the next day **(laughingly)** because we have a lot of work to do tomorrow morning, the Simpsons have some special guests for their garden party, but we might see you in the evening, we really would like to be here for the Tavern anniversary, naturally this will be after the show we are going to see at the Savoy Theatre, as we were given a couple special tickets, we don't usually see two shows as quick as that!"
"Yes you must come after that, you've got to sample one of our chef's specialities!"
"Thank you Don, we shall look forward to that. By the way Bob, can you settle the bill please, I'll see you later about that!" **(Don very prompt says)**
"It's all done my dear, it has been one of my greatest pleasures!"
"Oh no Don, you shouldn't do that, you are running a business here, your generosity is overwhelming."
"Nonsense Louise, I am the boss here, what I say goes..... I'll see you both tomorrow night, in the meantime I wish you both a good night!"
"Good night....Goodnight....Don!"

(Mary Louise and Bob leaves the Tavern)

"I say Bertie, what was all that commotion about?"
"Oh... nothing all that important Don, just a little family argument...."
"Just the same, I hope it wasn't very serious, you know very well that I wouldn't lose Lisa!"
"Don't worry Don... everything is okay now... **(And whispering)** between us and the four walls I think Joe is very jealous of Lisa, he hates people looking at her legs, and he doesn't like to see her smiling too much at the punters!"

"Nothing wrong with that Bertie!"
"I know that.. but you know jealousy is like a disease, and poor old Joe is affected by it!"
"Ah, ah, ah, ah I love that, he must be going bonkers... the old fellow!"
"Never mind Don, in life we go through something like that all of us, I'm sure you'd feel the same if you really love a special girl, I mean a special girl of your dreams!"
"You've got a point there Bertie, I think I would feel like that too!"
"See?? I'm glad you agree!"
"Unfortunately I do, I think I'd better start writing tomorrows duties, as it's going to be our big evening, and you make sure you write down what we need from our suppliers!"
"I'm just about to do it now Don!"
"That's my boy!"

(Don goes back to the bar to give a hand serving, while Bertie went back in the kitchen to make a list for the next day provisions)

"Ivy... please try and collect as many dirty glasses and plates as you can so they can wash them before the kitchen staff leaves!"
"Right oh... Don just leave it to me I'll be as quick as I can!"
"As soon as I finish what I'm doing I'll come and give you a hand!"
"Oh.... many thanks Bertie, you are ever so heplful!"
"Never fear.... Bertie is here!"
"Ah, ah, ah, ah.... I like that Bertie!"

Chapter 12

(The girls are back for some more singing and dancing. Joe's sitting at his table all on his own with an empty glass, while Bertie's collecting the last dirty glasses notices Joe talking to himself....)

"Hi Joe, come on mate, put yourself together it was only a silly quarrel, you don't really want to make it worse than it is."
"It's alright for you to say that, as you are not in the same situation as me!"
"Don't be so sure, I think my life is not better than yours Joe, just because you don't hear me arguing with Rosie, let me tell you my friend, we have our ups and down too like you!"
"You might be right.... but this time... Oh, I don't know what to say, I feel an idiot and in a complete muddle Bertie!"
"Perhaps a goodnight sleep will put your mind at rest Joe!"
"Hope you are right Bertie!"
"Of course I am right Joe, look at you...... you look like you lost a million dollars...."
"You mean a million dollars girl?
"That's alright two million dollars girl, and stop talking to yourself, tomorrow is another day, I'm sure you'll have new feelings about your sweetheart!"
"It's no use you know? Sometimes I really feel I don't love her anymore, and bloody good riddance. And another thing, since she started singing here, she thinks she's world's famous already, seeing all them perverts looking at her legs, it does annoy me a bit."
"Those are the first symptoms of jealousy...ha.ha.ha.ha."
"Okay you just laugh.... I am sure if were in my shoes you would think the same, so I will speak my mind as soon as I get home."
"You don't mean that Joe, you will only complicate the situation, it doesn't make any sense. Look at me, I am so happy, and I tell you something else, Rosie didn't come in tonight, where is she? Am I bothered? NO.. NO.. Who cares.. I couldn't give a toss!"
"Oh yes, you don't care because you eye up and down all them skirts, you know what? I think you are always on the lookout for a bit on the side, maybe you think that the grass is much greener on the other side, I am not like you... if you must know!"

Ah... you might not be like me but you are certainly very jealous, and that it's an unfortunate disease.... you can't stand seeing her being loved by her fans....Would you rather seeing her hated?"
"You must be joking... I am not jealous, me jealous? Not at all! Anyway I think she will pack her bags tonight, that's what she said, you mark my word Bertie!"
"Really.... Would you like me to put a good word in for you Joe, better still I don't mind asking Rosie, I'm sure she wouldn't mind doing it! You know girls talks communicate better!"
"Don't bother Bertie.... I don't love her anyway....and that's a fact!"
"Only trying to help you out Joe.... Oh, I better go back to my duties, I don't want to get the sack... furthermore we don't want the two of us be in the dog house.. that'll be funny, our friends will have something to say then!"

(It's almost closing time and nearly everyone's gone, Joe doesn't realize is that late as he starts looking at the small menu, perhaps he's thinking to order pie and mash as he hasn't had his dinner, perhaps he was too busy arguing with Lisa. All of a sudden the famous bell rings, that's alright the sign of closing time, looks at the old mother clock standing beside the counter.....)

"Goodness me, is that the time? Well I suppose I'll have to go home.... Hey Lucy... I can't see my other half, is she gone already?"
"Yes darling, she left an hour ago, she said she couldn't sing anymore tonight, so she asked to leave early, you really done your job alright, eh Joe? She must be proud of you!""
"Me? What have I done, I only expressed my feelings, sometimes you've got to say, what you got to say... to make yourself understood..."
"You have done that alright, she was very distressed, may I tell you!"
"I do not recall to have done anything nasty, except...."
"Don't excuse yourself, I guarantee you will feel sorry for yourself tomorrow, if you ask me she doesn't deserve it!"
"Is that's what you think Lucy?"
"Yes...Tch... men, I think I better be on my own..... Jane"
"Too right Lucy, they only mean trouble!"
"Thank you Jane!"
(Joe has no answer to that and walks over to Don)
"So sorry to interrupt you Don..."

"No problems dear boy, what can I do for you?"
"Well... I'd like to apologize, I think I've caused some problems tonight, I just don't know why I did it, I think I should keep my own problems in my own home!"
"Don't worry Joe, we all make mistakes now and then, just go home and have a nice cuppa, a good night sleep will get your mind fresh and ready for tomorrow's business!"
"Thank you and goodnight Don!"
"Goodnight Joe!"
(The bell rings again and a couple of times again)
"Tch.. One of these days I'm going to hang that bell around someone's neck!" **(Looking straight at Lucy)**
"Watch out what you say dear bruv, someone might hear you one of these days, then you'll be sorry, and it's about time you make your way home, if Rosie still up, tell her I shall be a bit late tonight, as I've got a few more things to organize for tomorrow's anniversary."
"Right... but I don't mind waiting for you, usually we walk home together..... I don't really mind, believe me!"
"I do believe you Pete....Don't worry about that, you know your way alright, I don't know how long I'm gonna be."
"By the way bruv.... how come Rosie hasn't been around this evening, did she have an evening out with a friend?"
"Why....... do you know something that I don't?"
"Not really, just asking, as I haven't seen her around this evening!"
"Look bruv... Rosie doesn't have to come to the Tavern every evening, she don't work here for that matter, and whatever Rosie does, it doesn't concern you at all!"
"As a matter of fact, it does concern me a bit, after all I am part of the family, I really wouldn't want to see you both being at each other's throats!"
"Shut up bruv, stop being a preacher in other's people affairs. I am married to her not you, you are just my silly brother, please go home."
"Sorry bruv, I didn't mean to interfere in your private life, it's only the fact that I care for you, and her too, it's one of my weaknesses!"
"Don't make laugh bruv...Although I appreciate your caring, but let me remind you that I'm old enough to care for myself! You seem to be doing it all the time, not only to me but to other people too, if you don't stop it, I will not be responsible to what will happen to you, perhaps I should find you a place in one of them work houses.....living in a room with ten mates or more, I wonder how you'd like that!"

"Okay, okay bruv... no need to be so nasty, I shall go now, anyway.. I've got to get up early in the morning to set up my stall, as I've got plenty bargains..."
"And try to behave yourself in that market, I am not very please what I hear..... and don't upset my mate Joe, he has enough problems as it is....
"Don't we know that??
"Yes I know.... you know.... you know everything....Good night Pete....
"If you say so bruv.... see you later...."
(As he goes out of the door Pete mumble to himself....)
"I'm not too happy about that, my rascal bruv he's up to something, as Rosie hasn't come to the Tavern this evening, something's odd, I'll find out tomorrow. I should have been a detective really!"

(**Another evening is over at the famous Tavern. Don is about to lock up, while Lucy's putting together a few props to take home to wash, and Bertie is just about finishing is ordering list for the next day**.)

"That's my lot, all done. How about you Lucy have you got all your staff together?"
"Yes Bertie, I think I've got everything, let me see now.. yes I've got my house keys!"
"Okay then let's go, I'll have to lock up the back door.. Goodnight Don **(shouting)** I'll go out by the back door!"
"Okay Bertie.... Goodnight.. see you tomorrow!"

Chapter 13

"Well... Here we are another evening's gone!"
"Oh, and what an evening we had, I just hope I am not going to dream about it, I think I will stay definitively single!"
"Yes we did, it was a very exciting evening, don't worry you won't dream about it, as for staying single are you sure Lucy....? What a waste, a beautiful girl like you, should not become a spinster... you've got to think of your old age, you'll be all alone, not a male to do the repair jobs, or to make you a cuppa when you are not feeling well.... can you imagine that?"
"Well... I think I never thought of that...."
"I just can see you sitting next to your coal fire knitting a jumper for your cat, if not an old dog!"
"Mind you, they are good company at least they don't argue, like husband and wife! On second thoughts I wouldn't say no to a good husband, and I'm sure the right one will come around!"
"See... one day you will thank me Lucy for my free friendly advice! Okay the doors are lock, and the lights are off! However, since we live in the same street Lucy, can we walk home together?"
"Why not Bertie, at this time of darkness a bodyguard can always come useful, not that I'm scared of anyone!"
"It's my pleasure, rest assure... I'm ready to fight anyone just to keep you safe, I like to be a hero!"
"Oh, that reminds me a film a saw not long ago."
"Oh yes? What was the title then Lucy?"
"I don't remember, I think it was a Rudolph Valentino one, he was always there to save his lady, what a good looking men he is!"
"That's true Lucy, he really knows how to treat ladies old Valentino!"
"But some of his films they make me laugh, they are too farfetched, the goody always wins, and gets the pretty girl."
"Oh, I really look forward to get home and murder a nice cup of coffee, but I suppose tea will do as usual, one thing though.... I'm always afraid to wake up Rosie, she really gets in a bad temper when I make too much noise."
"Tell you what Bertie, you can come in for a cup of coffee if you wish, after all we need to unwind after such an exciting evening."
"Oh, thank you Lucy... I do appreciate your kindness, must admit all we drink at home is tea, Rosie doesn't like coffee at all, between us, she's a proper east ender."

"Is she a cockney then?"
"I'm not sure she is, I wouldn't be surprised if she hadn't been born under the Bow Bells.... did you know though the people born in Cheapside are true Londoners?"
"Yes, I seem to remember my father mentioning that, but you know as kids you don't take much notice of that kind of history!"
"Cockneys are very proud of their history, because they say that they are the true English ones!"
"Well, here we are Bertie, street lighting is so bad around here, that sometimes it takes me five minutes to find the key hole.... there we are... please come in, you'll have to accept my humble residence as it is, don't expect a Royal palace..."
"Oh...Oh... but this is beautiful Lucy, and very, very cosy, so much better than ours."
"Well, sometimes I think it's too big for me, I've got three bedrooms, as I've got to think about my mum, when she visits me. She still lives in our old house in Leyton, she won't move out, mind you she's happy with her old friends she'd known them for years, and of course she likes to be surrounded by my father's memories, I keep some here, you know? Bless her she loved him so much, and I love her too!"
"Yes, I really like you taste, your decor is none but real first class, makes me wonder how you find the time to keep it so beautiful, I am very impressed!"
"You are too kind Bertie, I do appreciate your compliments, must admit apart from dancing and singing I like to decorate places, I think I have good imagination and fresh ideas, there again I work very hard to make it what it is."
"Perhaps you could become a painter and decorator, I haven't met any girl yet with that kind of inclination, I certainly can't see my Rosie painting our house!"
"Don't you kid yourself Bertie, there many women that can use the paint brush better than men! Maybe your Rosie can do it too!"
"You probably right, considering you have a full time job, you're brilliant, I must say!"
"Yes Bertie that isn't easy!"
"And the piano, not many houses have the piano now days, can you play it?"
"I struggle a little bit, as I passed my grades many years ago."

"You'll be able to replace Charlie then one day!"
"You must be joking....... I wish I was a professional like him though!"
"Well Lucy, I am simply flabbergasted, I can only say that if you ever decide to marry someone, you certainly don't need a house or a home, you already have your palace to live in!"
"That's a fine chance, to start I have no intention to get married, as I told you earlier I wouldn't mind to stay single, in saying that I haven't got a contestant yet.... so to speak!"
"You'll have no problems to find one. What? A beautiful girl like you, no problems at all!"
"There you go again on the same subject Bertie....but I like your compliments..... Go on sit yourself while I'll go in the kitchen to make some coffee!"
"Thank you Lucy, but if don't mind I'll have a pip at your kitchen too, I can imagine you have the latest gadgets, knowing you!"
"No Bertie, but please have a look... it's a normal kitchen really!"
"Well, well.. I give you full marks, I will only say this though, I wish I met you a few years ago, but then of course, you'd be only a kid!"
"Enough of this, I am not that much younger than you, maybe three or five years!"
"You are right Lucy you are five years younger than me!"
"How do you know that?"
"Don't forget I do the book keeping and the wages, so that's how I have all the details!"
"Anyway Bertie, now that we have sorted out the age problem, let me get on with my coffee!"
"Age doesn't mean anything Lucy, take Rosie for instance, she's only a year older than you and..."
"You mean I am lucky? If you say so!"
"No, what I mean is that age it's not that important.... darling Lucy!"
"Oh yes it is.... go on Bertie go and sit on the sofa, the coffee is nearly ready...."
"I don't mind anything stronger, if you have it!"
"Bertieeee, I said coffee and coffee shall be! By the way why don't you play that record already on the gramophone, I bought it today, it is from that famous band leader Harry Boy, you know he just married a Princess and he wrote that song especially for her, it's called "If I had a girl like you" he plays now at the May Fair Hotel in Berkley Square. Oh, some people say, they see them roaming around town in their luxurious automobile!"

"He must have a lot of dosh to afford that."
"Of course they have, she's a princess and he's a famous musician, my goodness Bertie, snap out of them clouds!"
"Sorry Lucy I'm still flabbergasted about your flat, it hasn't sunk in yet! I bet your bedroom is very matched with lovely feminine colours."
"Nice of you to say so, but I'm not showing you my bedroom it is quit private. I appreciate your compliments, and let me tell you that you are marvellous too in the Tavern, a lot of our regulars think the world of you, maybe it's your personality, you sure you know your job, it looks like you've done it for ages, perhaps that's why Don likes you a lot!"
"Many thanks Lucy, I'm only trying to do my best...... as for the bedroom it's only a compliment.. Ouch....I think this gramophone needs a bit of oiling Lucy, it's quite hard to wind up.... okay there...."
"Thank goodness you've done it.... nice sound isn't it?"
"Yes....Yes... not bad at all, it has a lovely sound and so clear.... I wish I had a gramophone like this one, they are so flipping expensive and the records.... they cost a fortune... no wonder these musicians go around with expensive cars!"
"I think they deserve it Bertie!"
"If you say so..... Goodness me look at your records collection, you've got enough here to play music all day long!"
"Yes I do have quite a lot, mind you they are all my father's, he did enjoy listening to his music after work, he always said that was the best way to restore his brains back to normal, as his job took out a lot of him... you can imagine being in charge of a railways station!"
"That was a big job, which station was he working for?"
"Victoria station....... that's it coffee's coming, there you are Bertie, sugar is beside you... I think you better stop the record, we don't want to wake the entire street, do we? Oh, I really treasure that gramophone, as you might know it belong to my father, I promised my mother that I look after it!"
"You know Lucy..thinking of that song, I wish I could write a song like that for the girl of my dreams, when I was gigging with Merlin and Joe, mind you Joe was with us only for a short while, we used to be quite a good duo, Merlin with his guitar, and me with an old battered pair of drums, with a couple of old sauce pans lids on top as the platters!"
"That must have been funny Bertie."
"Yes it was funny alright, because that was part of our act, and people loved it, in actual fact we could not afford a real drum kits!"

"I do admire you for that Bertie... you have a lot of dedication and good will, whatever you do! That's why your Rosie is crazy about you, and she's the girl of your dreams, so you don't need to write a song for any other one, okay?"
"You are probably right Lucy, but......"
"There's not buts..... Be sensible. Oh, I like Harry Boy, you know he plays the clarinet too?"
"No I didn't know that, in fact I didn't know much about him, not until you introduce his existence to me!"
"I would have thought you would have heard about musical personalities as you were yourself a musician?"
"Yes I was but for the past five years, I had so much on my mind, that I simply had no time for it, my estate agent job kept me very tide up to marital responsibilities, then along came the Tavern and with that I haven't had time to practice music at all, but after listening to Harry Boy, yes I would like to be like him, I might show you my musical talent one of these evenings at the Tavern."
"I will remind you that, I'll tell Charlie. Yes! Harry Boy I do like him very much myself, I like his style and his particular sound!"
"No need to tell Charlie, we done a few gigs in the past. Of course music styles keep changing Lucy, new big band sound is the in thing now!"
"Yes you are right, but although Harry Boy's band is only a sextet, I think he's great... Oh..I didn't know about you and Charlie!"
" Yes, I will say no more Lucy.... I've got an idea, as you like this Harry Boy so much, perhaps we could go and see him, have a nice dinner and a dance or two, naturally not for any particular reason, shall we say; as a token of a real friendship, how about it Lucy?"
"Bertieeee... it's nice of you to offer, but I don't really go out with married men, just imagine what people would say, that would really cause a scandal."
"If that really bothers you Lucy, I think there are ways to avoid certain gossiping!"
"No Bertie, I don't think it would appropriate, furthermore at the moment I don't intend to go out with anyone and I've got so many things to do. Why don't you take Rosie, I'm sure she'd be delighted!"
"I don't think she'd like that, beside she can't dance, imagine we'd be sitting at the table like two lemons, with very little conversation , and maybe ending up arguing... that's not the kind of cheering up I need at the moment!"

"What do you mean cheering up? I can't say that I've seen you miserable once, you're always smiling and quite content with your life, and......."

"That's where you are wrong Lucy...... Well, I was going to tell you, I suppose you'd find out sooner or later, no bones about....MY Rosie..... she's having an affair, she might even leaving me soon!"

"Oh Bertie... so it's true then? I thought that was just gossip going around, you know what it's like in the Tavern, your brother was spreading hints here and there as easy as you spread marmalade on a toast, his mouth will get the worse of him one of this days, have another cup of coffee, it'll do you good."

"Thanks Lucy for being so understandable, my bruv eh? He doesn't surprises me at all; luckily I haven't heard it from him. Why did she do it? I gave everything she'd wished for and to make it worse, she's having an affair with my mate Greasy, believe it or not!"

"That doesn't sound too good Bertie.... don't get yourself too workup. You'll see that very soon everything will turn out fine and rosie....so to speak!"

"Thank you Lucy for your good words, it's easier said than done, but life with Rosie, well... hasn't been all that rosie lately... so to speak!"

"True.... so to speak, ha, ha, ha, see? Nothing wrong to make puns out of problems or misfortunes, they can be mindful refreshing!"

"Perhaps I am entitle to make a joke too, after all she treated me like a joker more than once, making me feel good enough to patch up any holes, I always knew there was something wrong with her name.... Rosie.... Huch I presume it come from roses, the kind with a lot of thorns...."

"Now...Now Bertie, no need to exaggerate, I like Rosie and I like her name too. I think you were made for each other, she is your Rosie and you should be proud of her."

"You mean my ex Rosie!"

"No Bertie... YOUR Rosie, anyway, supposing she is really having this affair with Greasy I bet you wouldn't hesitate to have an affair yourself, maybe you already had one, go on be honest!"

"I'll be honest with you Lucy, I haven't had an affair as yet, but I've been thinking about it for a long time..."

"Haa.... you are hiding something you naughty boy!"

Chapter 14

(And so Bertie keeps on revealing his private idyllic confessions)

"Well, I am not hiding anything, I know I'm going to make a fool of myself.. (**holding her hand**) don't get me wrong Lucy, but I had my eyes on you for a long, long time, not for a galloping affair that is; but it's more than a soft spot, much more than that... I just can't stopped thinking of you night and day, you are becoming an obsession, if you only knew how many times I rehearsed these words. I love you Lucy..... I really love you. Goodness me I promised myself I wouldn't go this far! "

"Please Bertie don't muck about, we are two grown up human being , be serious.... anyway, I don't believe you. How many time do I have to tell you that you're a happy married man?"

"That is practically your opinion, if you only knew the truth.....Yes... you've got to believe me Lucy! Why should I lie? I see no reason to do that, certainly not to a good girl like you!"

"Gawd..... do you really mean that?"

"Of course Lucy... I really mean it from the bottom of my heart, it's hard to describe my feelings, what with working with you and being so near to you every evening, I just get frustrated watching you singing and dancing.... and... and... Yes I really get mad seeing you smiling at other men, I think I'm becoming like my mate Joe, you know he really gets mad sometime when Lisa smiles at someone else... so I get mad too... about you! I really feels like telling the world and...."

"But Bertie... I always thought that you fancied Lisa, you make so much fuss of her all the time!"

"That's where you are wrong Lucy! Okay I do make some fuss of Lisa, but only trying to get you interested in me... can't you see? Furthermore how can I fancy Lisa, I wouldn't really betray my best mate Joe, we've known each other for a long time and have been good friends since our school days... no...no I couldn't do that... and you know yourself Lisa is mad about him!"

"I do agree about that Bertie, Lisa said that many times that you and Joe are really good pals."

"And to say the least.. he's already asked me to be his best man at his forthcoming wedding, that says it all...... What more can I say?"

"You couldn't have been more specific. That's what I call real friendship Bertie!"

"I knew you'd understand me Lucy.. (**still holding her hand**) Now you know how I feel about you!"
"Oh.... Bertie.....**(Lisa starts trembling)** Do you really mean that? But...."
"There are no buts Lucy, if you only knew how many times I dreamt of you sleeping next to me... and when I wake up.... you are not there...."
"I suppose there's nothing to add to that Bertie....."
"Please don't say another word Lucy, let our hearts dictate our feelings, I love you so much, you are just adorable......Mmmm...!"

(Looking into each other eyes, a blinding love took over their feelings... they embrace and kiss passionately, Bertie looks high up with a sigh with a twinkle in his eyes as if to say; `tonight is the night Bertie boy` and so they carry on kissing and gently pushing Lucy on the sofa, but just as things seem to hot up, there's a knock at the door, both jump up feeling rather guilty, wondering who could that be at this time at night.)
"You'd better go and see who's at the door Lucy, whoever it is get rid of, we don't want anyone spoil our evening, shall I hide in the kitchen?"
"Why? You stay where you are my darling Bert.... We have nothing to hide, after all we have done nothing wrong... did we?? OH.. you are a darling...."
"Oh... I love that cheeky smile of yours Lucy... give us another kiss... oh, I could have you for dinner!"
"Oh darling, you'll have me for dinner another time......"
(Knock, knock) "Hawtch......Go on Lucy, can't you hear there's another couple of knocks....."
"Don't panic Bertie.... You look like as if you are guilty of something......Whoever it is... act normal!"
"Okay, I am normal but you know at this time anyone can aggravate the situation..."**(Knock,knock)**
"Okay, okay.. just sit there, make sure you have your cup in your hand, at least you can give an impression of drinking your coffee.... I'm coming, I'm coming!"
(Lucy opens the door and sees Lisa standing in the doorway with a suitcase)
"Lisa..... Don't tell me he has thrown you out!"
"No he hasn't... (**sobbing**) I left him, we started to talk and see if we could sort out amicably some stupid nonexistent problems, but he became very argumentative, so I told him I had enough... Oh, I feel so confused and exhausted!"

"Come on in Lisa and let off your steam, Bertie is here having a cup of coffee."
"I hope I am not intruding!"
"Don't be silly Lisa, Bertie and I thought to unwind over a cuppa, after such a long and tired evening, no need to tell you what it was like in the Tavern, forgive me to remind you that!"
"Don't worry Lucy, I don't mind you reminding me, it was the worst evening of my life, just don't know what came over my Joe!"
"He might have another woman, you don't know, but it's possible, I'm really sorry to see you in those circumstances, I wouldn't worry too much if I were you, I'm sure you two love birds will soon make it up!"
"Let's say no more about it Bertie, I think Lisa, had enough of those circumstances this evening, let's have another cup of coffee, do you want one Lisa or do you prefer a cup of tea?
"I would rather have a cup of tea if you don't mind Lucy!"
"Okay tea it is.... by the way, Bertie has been talking about you all evening... Don't worry nothing bad I can assure you!"
"Yes I did... I only mentioned that Joe was a bit unfair or shall I say out of order with you Lisa, which I think, you don't really deserve such treatment, after all you seem to be doing your share, when it come to take home a few pennies, and that makes you both equal... unlike my Rosie she earns peanuts, for the few little jobs she does... I'll say no more!"
"Thank you Bertie, I'm so glad that you sees it my way, I hope Joe will see it like you do and come his senses soon, if not it'll be really the end of our partnership and I am so sorry Lucy to bother you at this time, I am sure you don't need to hear somebody's else aggravations!"
(Lucy goes to the kitchen, but she comes back straightway)
"Oh, I've run out of milk Lisa, but that's no problem, I'll just pop over next door to borrow some from Betty, I can see her light from my window that she stills up, that woman works like a slave, since her husband left her for a younger one, thanks goodness she's good at her job, a damn good dress maker... **(and looking at Bertie)** Don't get up to anything I wouldn't do you two, won't be long, and give us a smile Lisa don't look so worried and miserable......"
"Don't worry Lucy, rest assured that Lisa is under my protection, I promise!"
"I trust you Bertie.... you are a gentleman!"

Chapter 15

"Good girl that Lucy, ehm... looking at your suitcase I presume you've come to stay with her, as I said before; sorry about your quarrel with Joe, I really think it was very unfair and rough the way he treated you, especially in front of your colleagues and more than anyone else he did upset Don, knowing that he thinks the world of you, that is Don, anyway, it's not up to me to criticise after all Joe is a good friend of mine, in saying that, he's blooming clever in his business, but I don't think he can deal with women.. **(shaking his head)** hasn't got a clue! On the other hand it seems to me we have the same problem, perhaps yours it's not as bad as mine, I expect you know about me and Rosie!"

"I did hear a rumour in the Tavern, but I have problems of my own to worry about, anyway, what happened Bertie? Hope it's not too serious, oh,,, I'm so fed up to hear about these arguments....still...."

"Well... to be brief I think she's having an affair with my good friend Greasy... tchh... call him good friend, that's a laugh.... maybe I am to blame... as we started drifting apart, not as bad as that, but our love was cooling down a bit, so to speak, of course I have been busy with the Tavern, so I believe I neglected her a bit, however, rascal old Greasy took his chance, the crafty bagger, I think he's had his eyes on Rosie for quite a long time, but since I am not the jealous type, I never took much notice, yes it was my job, working late every evening and she's been doing few part time jobs, that was the cause......Oh I really feel an old fool! But that's not the end of my life, she's got another thing coming!"

"What other thing do you mean Bertie? And I wouldn't call that friendship. Would you?"

"Please don't ask Lisa, you are so right, yes Greasy, you know we have been friends for years, and now he's probably laughing his head off, maybe my brother knew about that all the time, but he never mentioned it, he only talks when he shouldn't...."

"Maybe your brother didn't tell you because he didn't want to upset you, I believe he works down at the market with Greasy! Am I right?"

"Yeah... they have a stall near each other, and they both sell staff they can their hands on cheaply."

"Your brother seems to be doing alright to be a regular of the Tavern, How did you find out about Rosie?"

"Silly really, I was chatting to Percy this afternoon and this is what he saw and in his own words;

Apparently, Rosie helps out Joe when he goes for his break, at the same time Pete ask Rosie to keep an eye on his stall too, as he had to do a delivery, well.... Pete came back at the same time as Joe, then Rosie, started to chat very silently with Greasy, Percy said; intimately, hard to believe that, but I believe it now, then Greasy told his cousin Fred to mind the stall for a while, as the two of them share the same business, so Greasy and Rosie disappeared into the blue, no one seem to know the ending as Greasy never came back, because Fred had to pack up his stall all on his own!"

"Rather a complicated story... and a bit confusing... I'd say that Bertie!"

"Yes, Percy's story is a bit complicated but it has given me quite a few clues and to make it more real I didn't see Rosie all day long, and to prove it she was not in Tavern tonight, where was she...? And neither did I see Greasy around... what else can I say?"

"I bet Rosie will be awake just waiting for you...... with her open arms"

"I hope you are right Lisa, but I doubt very much, she's probably in the land of dreams, that is if she's at home... Oh I really feel like a blooming fool!"

"You are not a fool Bertie, I bet you a shilling that she's waiting for you with open arms!"

"I'll take your bet Lisa, what a coincidence, here we are the two of us in the same boat, but.... we haven't sunk yet, life is funny and full of surprises, we think we love someone, but we always end up choosing the wrong partner, in saying that I've got to bear a cross every evening looking at you in the Tavern and listening to some idiot treating you unfairly, if I may say so!"

"Yes you've got a point there Bertie.... I really felt very hurt and quite shocked, at his remarks!"

"I'm sure you did.....More than that Lisa, If you knew.... Good lord. Why haven't I met a girl like you before? So clever, good singing voice, gentle and very easy to get on with, you seem to have all the qualities for an honest, hardworking man like me deserves, unfortunately it never works out like that, we always end up marrying the wrong girl...**(and putting his on his heart)** if you only knew how I feel about you and....(**and looking up)** Good Lord.... I just don't know how to say this......!"

"But Bertieee... I think that.....You are exaggerating a bit, I'm sure your situation is not that bad!"

"Okay, okay... maybe I might have put my claim with a little bit of exaggeration... sorry Lisa... but this is how I feel and always felt about you since you started in the Tavern, or better still since I met you, I know, yes I know that we've been friends for a long time, but this doesn't prevent me to show you my feelings, and seeing you how hurt you are, I cannot hide those feelings any longer."

"Bertie I think you are saying these things because you are hurt about Rosie! Right?? "

"It's nothing to do with Rosie darling.... **(Lisa starts crying)** Oh, Lisa... don't cry... **(Bertie realizes and thinks, goodness me what have I done now?)** don't upsets yourself... it's not your fault... it's all Joe's, can't you see that? **(Bertie holds her sweet face with both hands and)** Go on give us a smile and... and...let me tell you the truth... I think that I'm falling in love with you!" **(Bertie thinks again this can't be real)**

(Looking into each other's eyes, Bertie seems to have hypnotized her, they embrace and their lips meet with a reassuring gentle kiss, sinking both their hearts into oblivion, unaware of everything else, in fact they don't even hear the door opening, naturally, it's Lucy coming back with the milk, she sees them kissing each other and......)

"Well, well..well.. as if my hospitality ain't good enough, nor is my coffee, by the look of things, I just don't know what to say... but I will say this Lisa; don't know whether to call you a trollop or a tart, you certainly didn't lose any time, perhaps Joe was right after all."

"Come on Lucy, Lisa is already upset as it is, really....surely you can overlook things like these.. no need to be mad like that, I was only comforting her!"

"Shut up you rotten swine, before I make a mince meat out of you and feed you to the dogs, or to the rats and let me tell you this; you don't comfort someone by throwing loving kisses about!"

(After this outburst Lucy sits at the table with her face in her hands crying, Lisa stands up and.....

"How could you **(crying too)** tell me that you loved me and kissed me.... I wouldn't be surprised if you had done the same thing to Lucy, I can see why she's so upset, yes very upset to deal with you... you devious man, and there I was falling in the same trap!"

"Well...I must admit I 'm a good hearted when it comes to conforting lovely ladies **(with a grin on his face)** You should be pleased about that, I shall bear no grudges!! All is forgiven and forgotten"

(**Lisa is just fuming**) "PLEASED....GRUDGES....FORGIVEN?? You lousy creep (**Lisa slaps his face**) This is from me! (**and again**) And this one is from Lucy, as she's too upset to deal with you herself!!"

(**Lucy gets up and...**) "Oh, you are so wrong Lisa, just watch me.... take that you big bully..(**and punches him right in his left eye)....** and some more to come if you don't get out of our sight...!

"Ouch.... Why did you have to do that Lucy? Lisa already gave me your whack!"

(**Lucy shouting**) "If you don't leave now, I'll give you a treble whack... YOUUUU little rat!"

"Okay, okay, I'm off, but don't think I will easy forget tonight. You both have been very unfair!"

(**Lucy slamming the door behind him**)

"Unfair.... bloody cheek, and good riddance to bad rubbish, shame will have to put up with him in the Tavern tomorrow evening!"

"Yes Lucy, but we'll have to make out as if nothing had happened, in fact no one must know that I came here so late tonight.... not even Joe knows that. Apart from the fact that Bertie knows, but I'm sure he will keep his mouth shut, otherwise you can imagine what kind of problems this will creates with Rosie and the gossiping with the rest!"

"You are so right Lisa, yes, no one must know what went on tonight, we don't want to be ridiculed from them lot! Mind you, I think I have given him a black eye"

"Well done Lucy.......Poor old Joe, you should have seen his face when I put the key on the table, he was utterly speechless, I guess he didn't expect to be left on his own that time of night!"

"You are right Lisa... must have been a shock for him...ha,ha,ha, forgive me for laughing!"

"Don't worry Lucy, I don't mind you laughing, to be quite honest I think he deserves that, I still don't understand why he had to behave like that in the Tavern! I've never seen him like that!"

"I know why Lisa, the answer is quite simple.... Joe loves you so much and for that he's very jealous, I think is even afraid you might find someone else, amongst the lot that comes in, you take it from me, Joe is not a womaniser like the one we just thrown out, your Joe will always be faithful to your heart... and no matter how many arguments you'll have you two, he'll always love you!"

"Thank you for your kind words Lucy, and your honest opinion.
However, if I hadn't come here in the first place, I'm sure this wouldn't

have happened, I feel I created this commotion out of nothing, I simply don't know what came over me.... but you were the first that came to my mind!"

"Don't blame yourself Lisa, in fact I'm glad you came, because this has given me the chance to see what kind of a man Bertie is made of!"

"Oh he's so crafty Lucy, he certainly knows his way around women, I really could see that he was trying his best to put the dagger into the wound, by criticizing Joe's character and how he treats me unfairly."

"Yes Lisa, I think that it is his favourite way to get what he wants with the opposite sex."

"And before I knew it Lucy, there he was holding my hands and my face, looking into my eyes and kissing me, I must say, he was very gently I thought... Yes I felt as if I was senseless or hypnotized!"

"Well... I am ashamed, but I must admit he did the same to me, perhaps he does have some sort of charm after all, I don't know whether to hate or feel sorry for him, in the end I think I still prefer Pete, good old soul, he might have a big mouth but deep down he's more trustworthy."

"Now I know, you keep torturing him in the Tavern, although you that he's madly in love with you, but he hasn't the courage to come out with it, you fancy him a lot, don't you? Come on be honest!"

"Perhaps I do Lisa! Just can't understand why he doesn't come out with it the little sod."

"Jolly good Lucy, I'm sure he'll make a good husband and of course the way you treat him, he will never tell you his feeling towards you, so be more gentle with him, that's the hints of a woman!"

"Now you are getting me too far ahead Lisa, I really haven't given a thought yet to be tight up with the opposite sex! But I will try to be more gentle with him... and call him Pete instead of Nosey!"

"That's what I like to hear Lucy! Anyway, what kept you so long from Betty?"

"She started telling me about her old man, and why he's left her for a younger woman, she was giving me a few tip about men, the funny thing was she warned me about Bertie, she said he's a bit of a womanizer, don't laugh, he tried it on with her sister in law, then she said very softly `he never got what he was after the rascal` I had to laugh at that... poor old Betty she also said that she didn't find it funny. If she only knew that Bertie was in my flat, drinking my coffee, in the company of two young ladies and making the fools of us..... can you imagine?"

"She wouldn't have given you the milk...ha, ha, ha, I suppose she's right to be upset in a way, after what she went through with her husband shacking up with a younger bird!"
Too right, I would be upset as well Lisa! We seen enough tonight what one man can do!"
"Thank God it's all over now, and I don't really feel sorry for him..... Now Lucy are sure you don't mind putting me up for a couple of nights, while I look around for somewhere else?"
"No problem my good friend, I always keep a spear room for my mother, and tonight is yours, in the morning I will give you a spear key, but I hope to see you back with Joe, he loves you tremendously!"
"I am ever so grateful, I won't forget your kindness, you are a real good friend Lucy!"
"Don't mention it, perhaps I should be the one to thank you again, it's a real pleasure, good night Lisa!"
"Goodnight Lucy!"

(Lisa goes to her bedroom and looks out of the window, looking at the starry skies and thinks; `Joe... what have we done? We were so happy! I wonder if you'll be thinking of me, I really do miss those evenings when we used to hold hands and kiss me so tenderly, yes my heart still beats for you.... I love you so much...and she starts softly humming his favourite song; `If I would give my heart to someone`)

Chapter 16

(Early morning, the sun is making its daily appearance on the local market, the traders seem to be very busy setting up their stalls. It's not a very big market but considering its size it has a lot to offer, the vendors are quite pleasant, amongst the many we have Joe doing his best to get over his love life, surrounded by Nosey Pete, Greasy, Fred, Stan and Percy the stutter and a few others, it is a joy to hear them shouting their advertising jingles for the first half an hour, naturally to get the buyers attention.)

"Roll up, roll up, come and get it, all local grown, fresh and crispy, enough to make you frisky."
"Where else can you get a better bargain? Only on Pete stall you can find them all."
"Come and try the latest fashion, pure cotton and Shetland wool all for your kiddies' school."
"Listen to thhhhe wonderful soooound of mmmy own bbbreed, from bbbirds to chicks and cockerels too.... with all the cocхарактерcolours just for you!"
"Blamey Percy... why don't you keep your jingle a bit shorter? That would make easier for the people to understand you!"
"Sssshut up Nosey... it's nnnnot my fffault if I ssstutter!"
"Watch your mouth Pete, and stop discriminating the handicaps!"
"I dododon't think you're vvvery ffunny Stannnley!"
"I'm only taking your side Percy! Hey...... anyone knows what happened to Greasy? It's not here this morning... I think I'd better ask Fred, he probably knows more than us....!"
"Maybe he was too busy entertaining a member of my family, ah, ah, ha, ha!"
"Shut up Nosey.... and mind your own business..."
"I'll say no more Stanley and I will ask no more questions to Percy on that matter....!"
"You better nnnot Nooooszey!"
"You seem to be well informed Percy on that matter... tell us more!"
"Mmmy lips aaare seallled!"
"Thank you Percy... and will you stop bickering you lot, you are a disgrace to my good customers."

"Well said Joe, let us have my order please..."
"Come and get my goodies, my loving treasures, all for a penny a pound.... and thank you to you my darling sweetheart, here's your change....Good morning Carolina, here you are my love, pound of apple for you, nice tomatoes this morning and crispy cabbages... there are only two pence each thanks mam, so glad you brought your own bag... Hello Mrs May..."
"There you are again Joe. You keep forgetting my name...."
"So sorry darling, it's them lot over there they are confusing me... Thank you Angelina, here's your pound of pears.... would like anything else?"
"Thank you my love..... That'll be all."
"Never mind Angelina, I was first you cheeky Joe...... you know we all love him!"
"Thank you Carole, you're a sweetheart, and I love all too!"
"Why don't you save your sweet words for your lonely nights, Joe?
"Why don't save your energies and shut up again Nosey?
"Sorry Joe give us a smile..... OH....... good morning Greasy you are late this morning, what happened, good job you've got your cousin Fred to keep the business going?"
"Oh, I had to go up the council to get my new licence..."
"Did they give you one Greasy? A licence for what? I better not comment about that!"
"Say another word Nosey and I'll give you one on your head... you cheeky basket!"
"Tch... can't you take a joke? Or are you upset about something or other... maybe the other!?"
"Shut your mouth Nosey........
"Sorry Greasy!"
"You certainly can get rid of your goods Joe, how do you do it?"
"Gift of the gab, that's what he's got Stan."
"Not certainly like your Nosey."
""Oh yes... and what do you mean by that Stanley?"
"I mean that you've the gift of the GRAB...ha,ha,ha,ha."
"I don't think that's funny."
"Well.... I'm sure many of your so called friends in uniform don't find it funny Nosey."
"Okay Stan, if you are so clever, what are you doing around here then?"
"I'm here to keep my eyes on you boy."

"Not with your brains Stan! If you must know I've got it all up here and I use it right when I needed, **(Pointing his finger to his brains)** That is something you ain't got."
"Keep quiet Nosey you are disturbing my customers!"
"Me quiet? You must be joking Joe, what about Percy's birds then? they never shut up, Ohy Percy shut them birds up."
"Mmmmaybe they aare trying tocccopy your bbbig mmmouth Nosey."
"Oh ssshut up Pppercy!"
"Stooop taking the mmmickey Nosey...."
"Watch out Pete here comes the ol' Bill...."
"Why can't they mind they own flipping business?"
"Why? I'll tell you why Nosey, if you'd be more honest the ol'Bill wouldn't be sniffing around here!"
"Oh, Yeah? If we were all honest in this world they'd be out of a job, right clever Joe?"
"You better shut your gob Nosey, he might hear you."
"You can shout Joe, you didn't shut yours last night in the Tavern, did you?"
"Count yourself lucky that I'm very busy or I would knock that big head of yours off.... Nosey"
"Okay Joe, there's no need to get annoyed, you did shout a bit last night!"
"Be quiet Nosey.... You don't need to tell the whole world""
"Okay...okay... Joe....(**And looking at Stan)** What are you hiding Stan?"
"I've got nothing to hide mate, I wonder about the staff you sell if it could talk you'd probably end up as a guest of his Majesty!"
(**Stan grabs Nosey by the neck and gives him a wallop, as the ol' Bill is just about to appear)**
"Hello, hello... what's going on here?"
"Nothing officer, he said something nasty about me sis, and I stuck for her, he actually said that she's got two boyfriends.. bloody cheek!"
"That's alright officer, it's the truth, poor old Nosey.... got quite a crush on young Tessa... **(and whispering to the ol' Bill)** it's not his lucky day today, he's a bit superstitious as it is Friday the thirteen... you know what? this morning he put salt in his tea instead of sugar, ha,ha,ha,ha,ha!" He hasn't stopped drinking water!!"
"Mind your flipping business Joe!"
"Now, now, calm down Peter, you are not the only one who's got problems, you know?"

"Why... have you got problems too ossifer... pardon me... officer!"
"I don't like your sense of humour today Peter, I'm only trying to be sympathetic!"
"You are wasting your time officer, he doesn't know the meaning of the word sympathetic!"
"That's where you are wrong Greasy, I know what he means our good friend, is only expressing sympathy to my great and good personality!"
"Oh, oh.. we are getting clever, maybe you are getting some grammar lesson from some female teacher!"
"That's right Greasy, I have a female teacher, she's single and beautiful too, the other thing is... I don't go around stealing someone else's wife....!"
"Shut your trap Nosey... you talk too much!"
"Now, now then enough of your bickering, just remember that I am on duty, and my duty is to keep the peace and order around here, I will not put up with arguments!"
"Sorry about that officer but Nosey was accusing me for something which I didn't do!"
"Well.. I don't really want to interfere in family matters, unless of course the problem becomes serious, let me remind you that our accommodation is still free, in fact we have some empty cells!"
"Thank you officer, I rather live in my own accommodation and I will deal with him later!"
"Now then Greasy, there's no need to be too anxious about revenge, there are limitations, you know? And don't worry about our empty cells they are only for murders!"
"Alright sergeant, i will let him survive for the time being...."
"Now let us see, the other reason I am here it's because the other night there was a robbery at the old vicarage, so this morning I shall have to check your stalls, just in case someone came around to flog you some of the stolen goods, no offence!"
"Would we do that.... officer we would never accept anything but legal goods, that is from honest traders.... like ourselves....!"
"Well said Greasy, you took the words out of my mouth!"
"That's the least I can do Pete to show the officer that we are all honest around here!"
"Well... in that case I shall start from you Peter!"
Please help yourself officer, I certainly would not sell stolen goods from the local vicarage... ME? I am a devout Christian and a regular church goer!"

"That's a laugh, his only church is the Piccadilly Tavern, that's where he can watch them beautiful dancers and their legs... **(looking at Joe)** Sorry Joe but Lisa's got beautiful legs too!"

"I'll second that!"

"Shut up Nosey....(**looking at Stan)** Don't worry mate you can say what you want about Lisa, I can't be bother with her any longer!"

"Okay Peter... you are in the clear... I shall do the rest now...."

(**The officer finished his checking and is about to leave)**

"On behalf of the law, I thank you my friends for your good cooperation......**(As he walks away)** Yes, this is new to me... superstitious, Friday the thirteen salt in the tea instead of sugar..ha, ha, ha,ha. I like that, I bet my fellow officers will find it very funny, can't wait to tell them!"

"Yes I think it's funny we all like it too... salted tea.. and we like to be here to serve King and Country.. **(and whispering)** sarcastic basket"!

One of these days he'll catch up with you Nosey, then you'll be sorry!"

"Never you mind Joe, you seem to be sorry for yourself about something or other!"

"One more word from you Nosey and you'll be really taking a day off, you better start minding your stall, for what I can see you are not selling a lot today, (**and whispering in his hear)** and stop telling stories about Lisa, I think I've had enough of your gossiping!"

Chapter 17

(Unbeknown to Joe a lady customer was waiting to be served)

"So sorry Madam, good morning to you, what can I do for you?"
"Good morning to you young man, please don't apologize, I noticed that you were dealing with a rather obstinate young man, my name is Miss Ryan and this is my list, I would like this order please, my chauffeur will pick it up and settle the bill in half an hour, I would appreciate if I can get it ready in time by then, may I recommend you that they are all fresh, as they will be used this afternoon?"
"That'll be no problem Miss Ryan... thank you Miss..."
"By the way, I think I saw you in the Piccadilly Tavern last night, my friend and I popped in for a glass of bubbly, and luckily we met the landlord who I hadn't seen for years, we used to be good friends, you know? Incidentally, we were very impressed with the young singer, very charming girl, I saw her in the market earlier and I congratulated her for her good singing, she introduced herself as Lisa, that is her name, isn't it? I guess you know her, do you like her voice too?"
"Yes that is her name... and we know each other, naturally, she has a beautiful voice too, she's really good! By the way, I shall put a couple of bunches of fresh parsley with your order if you wish!"
"Yes please, that's very kind of you, that'll come handy for our buffet, and thank you for your good service, sorry I didn't get your name...."
"Joe... is my name.... just Joe..."
"Short and easy to remember Joe.... no doubt we shall meet again soon... goodbye for now!"
"Goodbye and thank you mam..... Miss Ryan.... see you soon again...I hope!"
(Talking to himself)
"What a charming lady, good looking too and what a personality! Old friend of Don? Just can't believe it, crafty little Irish, maybe I should have told her that Lisa and I are in a relationship or we were, what difference does it makes? No difference at all, anyway, I better get that order in boxes, goodness me there's enough groceries here to feed fifty people....Maybe she's got a big family

(Merlin the busker makes his monthly appearance on the market, a very good spot for him to make a few pennies with his guitar)

"Good morning Peter, are you well?"
"Oh... Good morning Merlin, I am okay, I'm sure you're okay too, is the other half that I'm worried about, anyway, we've been waiting for you to cheer us up, **(looking at Joe)** we got so much misery around here lately, I think I'm gonna cry....!"
"Don't listen to him Merlin, sometimes he doesn't know what to say anymore...."
"hello Joe... how are you? I see you are very busy filing up boxes, I guess you have a big order, business must be good then..."
"Can't complain Merlin..."
"How about you Peter? I hope your business is prosperous too, today!"
"Not bad, not bad at all, could be better today, if anything this morning we had the law checking our goods, and of course, customers don't like to see the coppers around here!"
"Well, I suppose they'll have to do something to earn their wages.....I haven't seen your brother Bertie lately, maybe is the married life that keeps him busy!"
"You can say that again Merlin, you know, only the other day he was telling me about the good times you had the two of you, when you were gigging together, and that's going back only five years I believe. However, I think he'll be around later!"
"Yes you are almost right Pete, I think just over five years, we were very happy, although we didn't make a fortune, but we didn't have as many bills coming in as we were young and bachelors!"
"Of course you are married too, how is your other half?"
"Carolyn is well, thank you Joe, she has a small job and she looks after our little house, as you know we live in Brighton now, but soon we shall start to do our usual gigs around the South East Coast, that will help to pay the little mortgage we took out for the house."
"Very sensible if you ask me, us at the moment we are renting, your mate Bertie will be around very soon checking if the grass is greener on the other side."
"Don't believe too much what our fried Joe says.. Merlin, my bruv loves his wife a lot!"
"I know that Pete... but I think he's a bit jealous of her beauty
"Yes I know, never mind, I know somebody's else that suffer that kind of desease.... but the good thing is that you are still with us. Set yourself up Merlin, while I'm going to get you a pint of good Ale and some grab, I'm sure you'll be hungry by the time you finish your first song... I am a

bit peckish myself too! Keep your sound nice and smooth!"
"Thanks Peter... I shall do my best!"

(So Merlin starts his first song, he's a real master with his guitar.... he sings the right one to make sure that he can collect a few pennies and is; `I've got no money`)

`I've got no money/But I'm so lucky/I've got the whole world/I.ve got a sweet girl!/No one will ever replace her/She'll be my one forever/Someday my dream will come true/Cos' my heart is set on you!/I've got no money/Don't care for honey/I care for you girl/You are my whole world/You make my life so wonderful/You are so nice and beautiful/You're number one from the start/No one will break us apart!.... No I don't need any money/Cos' you're sweeter than honey/You'll never, never, be blue/Please let me say; I love you....I love you....I love you!
(Pete is back with Merlin's grab)
"You really made my day Merlin, your great sound and your good voice reached `The Fat Duck` the landlord appreciated your song so much that it wouldn't take any money, when I told him that it was for you.. here warm yourself up with this pie and mash and wash it down with this good English brew, you really waste your time around here... when will someone recognize your talent..?"

(Rosie just showed up from the corner shop where she does a few part time hours.)
"You are right Nosey, he's got more talent than you have and some others!"
"Oh yes...? Perhaps you are one of the very few who does not recognize my hidden talent, if you were in the Tavern last night you would have witnessed my performance followed by a standing ovation from the crowd, you can ask anyone who were there, ain't that right Joe?"
"Yes... yes... if that makes you happy!"
"I am glad I wasn't there, on second thoughts, I'll be in tonight, if you'll do a replay I might even clap you... after all it's going to be the big night for the Tavern!"
"I'll see what I can do.... dear sister in law....."
"Yes, and you sister in law would like to know where Bertie is.... have you seen him by any chance?"

"Yes he popped around earlier, and said that he'll be around after dinner...."
"You mean lunch... you twerp... dinner is tonight!"
"Okay, okay... I meant lunch, how many people around here can tell the difference between lunch or dinner? We are almost all east enders my darling sister in law, not stuffy continentals, therefore there's no need to be so stuck up. Any messages for your sweetheart if he comes, just in case you are not around? **(and whispering)** by the way, what's up with you and old Greasy then?"
"Oh him... don't shout too loud, he might hear you... I'll tell you something Pete, he is as bad as all you men...you are all the same, when you are in trouble you always end up asking the opposite sex for help..... if he comes around tell him I'll see him later, he knows anyway that I was working at the `Needles & Cottons` store, so there'll be no problems! And don't ask me anymore silly questions about Greasy, we don't want people to get the wrong impression... do we?"
"Okay, I only ask you because you and Greasy disappeared for the whole afternoon yesterday..."
"We went for a cuppa, if you must know and then he ask me advice about his personal problems, naturally, he wouldn't ask his friends for fear to be ridiculed, when I left him I met my younger sister Eve, and we ended up at my parents house for another cuppa and stayed for some dinner, before I realize.... we spent the whole evening chatting away... that is the reason why I wasn't in the Tavern last night, are you satisfied?"
"Fair enough Rosie, I didn't really want to make a drama out of it... it's the other half, who's got dirty minds, and to be honest I do care about my brother and you, as you are both nice to me....sometimes, primarily because you let me stay in your house, and I'm grateful for that!"
"Yes... Considering you are a bit of a rascal sometimes, but we like to have you, although I feel like you are my son sometimes, but God knows if your brother and I will have any...one like you.... I hope not... God help us... no offence Pete!"
"Not so nice to hear that Rosie, but I would be glad to be uncle to one like me, in saying that, the girls have missed you too in the Tavern last night, and of course myself!"
"Missing me, not you? I don't remember the last time you bought me a drink? And, talking about problems.... For a start you don't have to worry about our problems, we can deal with ourselves, on the other

hand you better look after yours for a change, as you don't seem to be short of!"
"If you must know Rosie, I've got no problems, my very few are from the people who despise me, good job I've got a few girls who admire me!"
"That's another laugh, let me hold my ribs, I can't take this any longer, will you ever change? I'll tell you something my dear brother in law, you'll be so lucky to find one that put up with you!"
"You are exaggerating Rosie... there are hundreds out there, waiting for my proposals"
"No, I am not, and tell me another thing; why did you walk home on your own last night? And why was he so late?"
"I can only answer the first question, I couldn't wait for him because he was organizing the staff duties and the list for the next day anniversary, the rest I cannot tell you, is that fair enough Rosie?"
"Fair enough... for a change you sound more honest than usual... thanks a lot!"
(Joe who's been listening burst out laughing)
"Ha, ha, ha, ha, ha, I like that Rosie you reminded of one of them crimes detectives... anyway, can you please keep an eye on my stall while I take a break, my stomach is rumbling for my usual bacon sandwich!"
"Just leave that to me Joe, you go and have your break in peace!"

"Thanks Rosie... Oh I really liked your last comment about Nosey and his women...ha,ha,ha,ha, see you later, I won't be long! Greasy come on and have a cuppa with me, Fred can look after the stall alright."
"That's a good idea Joe, nice to get away from these lot for a change..... for a bit of peace... see you later Fred!"
Rosie decides to give a little advice to the rest of the vendors;
"Right..... Now boys listen here, while I mind Joe stall I would like to give you all a little advice, actually you can call it a sermon if you prefer.... Merlin you can follow me with your guitar, strumming a few chords.......
"Rosie do you know the musical key you'll be singing this.....?"
"I don't know what you are talking about...I can only tell you that it goes like this "La, la la, la, la, la, la, la, la, la, and la, la, la, la, la,...... got it?
"Yes Rosie.... I'll make it easy for you, I'll play only a few chords....you can start if you wish....

Chapter 18

(Rosie starts her sermon, practically in honour to her husband)

"If I had my way in this world mates/ I would casturate quite a few/I would not quite simply hesitate/Starting from the baddies like you!?If I had my way in this world mates/I would trash that old mate yours/I would see that he never talk soft/Quite unfairly with old Rose!

I just offered him my kind opinion/to go back to his gentle sweetheart/But he made me a good proposition/Stay with me Rose and we'll never part!"

If I had my way in this world mates/I would stand my man on a leg/He would come to terms and appreciate it/Then it would the best man I had!

(**Unbeknown to Rosie, Bertie was standing on the corner listening to every word she sung so far, so he walks to her and gives his reply:)**

If I had my way in this world mate/No wife would have done what you did/Even if you thought to be really great/By helping a good friend in need!

I know you gave your opinion/You knew well he was not asking that/I am sure he was under illusion/If I'm wrong I will eat my best hat!

Both: Yes we do like to have our own way/But sometime it isn't like that/You could be right but let me just say/You'll have to eat your own best hat! ---

There are a million things we ought to know/Wish we could all have our own way -- in this world!"

"Wonderful both of you, you should be on stage at the Victoria Palace..... and I like the song, did you write it Bertie?"

"Yes, but with the help of my boss...**(pointing his finger at Rosie**) we wrote it on our honeymoon in Blackpool... those were the days my friend!"

"Don't talk rubbish Bertie, you are still consuming your honeymoon!"

"Too right Merlin, he doesn't know how well off he is, you take it from Rosie!"

"Don't believe every word she says Merlin, she can exaggerate sometime!"

"Maybe that is your opinion! You've got a lovely girl there Bertie."

"If you say so Merlin,..... Rosie you have a customer!"

"Sorry about that madam, what can I do for you?"

"Thank you, I'll have a cabbage and three pounds of them spuds!"

"Right.. oh.. mam....
"That was a very good backing Merlin, I must say you are getting better and better
"I really did enjoy it myself too Bertie, it was a great pleasure, I do like Rosie's voice, not bad at all!"
"Don't tell her that Merlin, she'll want to go now on stage too. However, How are you Merlin?"
"Not bad Bertie, nice to see you too, I've been touring up North, as a replacement to a couple of bands, but unfortunately I never got a job that I would call steady, still, I can't complain as long as I earn enough for my bread and butter... You know something.... I earn more money by buskin than playing in a band goodness me I've never seen you with dark glasses!"
"Well..... I have to wear them to relax my eyes, as I spend most of my time in that Tavern with poor lighting... still is a job!"
"Come Bertie you know you like that job, and the owner thinks the world of you!"
"That's true... he looks after me alright!"
"Pardon me Bertie... that little argument between you and Rosie, are you both okay? I know it's none of my business, but I'd be sorry to see you both splitting up, to me you are just the perfect couple, and between us.... I think she's a very clever girl!"
"We just had a misunderstanding Merlin, the usual quarrel between husband and wife!"
"So glad to hear that... you are not the only one..... well, I think I'll start to get my gear together, I have another gig late this afternoon and one tonight!"
"Good gracious you are busy, where are tonight then?
"In Leicester Square... I'll be playing with a mate of mine, the named is Mario, he's an Italian, and he plays the Sax. He's pretty good he can do wonderful improvisations, these Italians are good when it comes to music, and I say that from popular to classical as well as opera!"
"Yes... I hope it goes well for you both, if you can spear the time tonight, pop in the Tavern for a quick drink.... okay see you later Merlin.
"I'll try my best Bertie....Bye for now."
(Joe's just back from his break with a pleasant smile on his face)
"Thank you Rosie, I'm ever so grateful for your help!"
"Don't mention it Joe... it's nice to hear the word `Grateful` that's more than I get from someone else....**(looking at Bertie)** Bye, bye Joe, see

you later!" **(Rosie walks away without saying bye-bye to Bertie... who finds himself rather embarrassed towards Joe)**

"Oh well, I think I better go and get ready for work, I think it's going to be a very busy evening! I see you this evening Joe, that is if you are coming to the Tavern!"

"Of course I'll be there Bertie, I can't miss this special night, I even might get a free drink, to celebrate the Tavern first Anniversary!"

"I'm going to make sure that you'll get a free drink Joe, actually I can't promise that you'll get a free smile.... if you know what I mean!"

"Well.... fancy you saying that.....I've got a feeling that there will be two fellows not getting any free smiles tonight...... Bertie!"

"You could be right there Joe.... so we'll have to play our cards very carefully....."

"I'm sure you will play your cards carefully Bertie, you seem to be good when it comes to cheat!"

"I will not comment on that Joe.... See you later!"

"See you later Bertie!"

(In the meantime in Lucy's flat the two girls were trying out a couple new numbers before going to the Tavern)

"Good lord Lucy you are so good playing that piano, I never knew that, I think if you practice a bit more you would be as good as Charlie!"

"Nonsense Lisa, I know I passed a few grades, but I wouldn't there to try to be as good as Charlie!"

"Anyway, I think that we know the routine now, all we have to do is to repeat it with the other girls!"

"That's alright Lisa with Charlie there will be no problem because he can read the music!"

"True... I really would like to see or to be able to read Joe's mind, and wondering where I went at that time of night!"

"He might think that you got a taxi, and and went back to your parents!"

"That's a good idea Lucy, I think he might ask you tonight, if you know where I ended up last night!"

"Alright Lisa, if he ask me I will say that you have gone back to your parents for good, he's bound to ask!"

"Please Lucy... say that, and later on after I had a chat with Don, I might let you into a secret which no one knows!"

"Come on then tell us... don't keep me in suspense!"

" I can only say that it's about a job's offer, I'll say no more, let's wait!"

Chapter 19

(In a few hours the Piccadilly Tavern will open once again its doors for a joyful evening of songs and dance, but tonight is going to be a very special night for Don and his staff. Charlie the piano player has been rehearsing new songs for a few hours, Lucy and girls are there too, getting their dancing routine to perfection. Bertie is also around in his blue waist coat with a red bow tie.)

"Good evening Bertie have you been here long?"
"Good evening Don, just a couple of hours, actually I've been stacking up some bottles on the shelves in the cellar!"
"My God what's happened to your eye?"
"Nothing much Don, I just had a little accident in the cellar, unfortunately one of the bottles fell on my eye from the top shelf, I was lucky really, I could have lost my eye, good job I was in time to avoid the worse! If I may mention to you I think we need better lighting down there!"
"You're probably right, and I will see to it, but dear old boy, you can't work in those conditions tonight, I think I'd be better call in John, I'm sure he can replace you at a short notice!"
"No need for that Don, I am okay really!"
"Nonsense, you do as I say, and that's an order, I think a good evening off it'll do you the world of good, and if you wish you can hang around as a customer!"
"If you say so, that's very kind of you Don!"
"After all Bertie you have been working too hard lately...."
"Okay Don, but if you really need me I will work.... or I can help out in the kitchen, as a standby!"
"Don't insist Bertie, only if it is an emergency, you take the night off, for now we got enough staff in the kitchen, furthermore we don't want our customers to think that you have been involved in some fights here in the Tavern, that would look bad for business!"
"You've got a point there Don, I do agree with you, one hundred per cent.

(Charlie and the girls have just left for their supper meanwhile Bertie is hanging the little British flags around the walls, when two delivery men come in with a few boxes..)

"You can put them there boys, and thank you very much!" **(giving them a little tip)**
"What's in them Don?"
"HAAA... just the job.....I was waiting for those, I thought for a moment they wouldn't arrive in time, look, just look at them Bertie.... That's alright these are new records made by the well known "Singalong" record company, you remember when Mercury Radio came to interview the girls and Charlie, they made a couple of recording, well, I managed to convinced Singalong with a little arrangement that will favours us all to produce these two recordings on record...which from tomorrow they will be available in all records shops in the Country.... As you can see, on one side we have `Love and Champagne` and the other side we have `If I would give my heart to someone` while the girls and Charlie are having their supper, you can make a nice exhibition on that stand I provided and stick them posters with the artists photographs and price, we have one hundred here to get rid of tonight!"
"I am speechless Don, I don't think you sleep at night, you are a good business man, if I may say so!"
"Thank you Bertie.. forget the compliments, get down to assemble the records before them lot come back.... I just look forward to see their faces... I am so happy Bertie, this gives me a lot of satisfaction, it's not so much the money you know? It is simply the creation of something new or shall I say simply an achievement! Plus Charlie, Lisa and the girls they deserve lot of appreciation!"
"Indeed they are very good Don, and they managed to print a little picture on the cover!"
"That's the idea Bertie, it means more free advertising for the Tavern, not that we need it really!"
(John just arrived) "Good evening Don, Oh hello Bertie..Oh.... they are nice, new records eh? what happened to your eye Bertie? I hope that wasn't Rosie......who did that!"
"Hi John, thanks for coming at short notice, I appreciate that, but for the record, not for that record, if you see what I mean, Rosie didn't do that, it was simply an accident...I can't believe it, everyone thinks Rosie punched me in the eye, I can assure everyone that no woman ever did punch me!
"It was only a joke, no offence Bertie believe me....But I like the record joke, I see what you mean!"

"Oh I know John... don't worry, I know you didn't mean it, Nice to see you anyway, you're always there to save the bad situation!"
"Ha.... I better go upstairs and get myself ready, I'll have a nice soak in my new bath first! Pity I miss the girls reaction, I was looking forward to that, but you'll tell me later Bertie!"
"I will Don rest assure... you have a nice soak, you'll be as good as new when you come down!"
"You are right Bertie it is a nice bathroom I've got, it's really well designed, fit for a king, thank goodness it's completely finished, must admit they have done a very good job!"
"A bit of luxury won't hurt you Don."
"I think I deserve it, what the hell, I worked blooming hard and I'm still working like a slave, why not? See you later Bertie."
"See you later Don...."

(The girls and Charlie arrive and they are flabbergasted when they see their new record exhibited next to the stage. Once again the Tavern open its doors with the usual sound of their signature tune of `Love and Champagne` the well know Charleston, the place is filling up quickly. Ivy the waitress stands at the door offering a glass of Madeira to everyone coming in and Jane's walking around with a silver platter of little pork pies and a few other bits for the customers to sample. Brenda is very busy taking orders for the diners, and serving behind the bar.
The menu is very simple consisting of; Pie and mash, Fish and chips, beer battered haddock and black pudding and potatoes cakes, Irish beef pie cooked in Ale, Pork belly with Irish stuffing, braised faggots with potatoes cooked in cider, some cold platters and some other dishes and various puddings.)

(The crowd seem to enjoy them beautiful dancers according to their applause, Joe is sitting quietly at a small table next to the stage.)

"Hello Joe, here's a pint of our best Ale with Don's compliments and wishes you a very pleasant evening!"
"Oh many thanks John and will you please thank Don, it is very much appreciated... and nice to see you here, I am surprised, it's not your usual evening, what happened to Bertie then, I haven't seen him around!"

"Oh he's around alright, I'm only here because Don gave him the night off, at the moment is up in the office tiding up some paper work."

"Lucky fellow that Bertie, I do envy him, he has almost everything a man could wish for!"

"Come on Joe, you shouldn't complain, you've got a good business too and a beautiful girl friend and very clever I must say, she's a terrific singer, a good dancer and with a great personality!"

"Well John, sometimes it's not all what it may seems, we think we have everything in life but all of a sudden we find that there's something missing, for instance, I was reflecting on that song `Love and Champagne`..... But I suppose you are an old married man, and you are happy too in your little world, in saying so, I shall let you go behind your bar and thank you again for the Ale!"

"Yes, I am quite happy, I have a lovely family and a good job, can't ask for more! See you later Joe!"

"See you later John! Yuck... Love and Champagne (**approaching Charlie)** Yes Charlie, two different words but they certainly have something in common, too much of either of them.. makes your head go round, take champagne for instance; easy come easy go, that is if you got plenty of dosh, not to forget that it could become a very expensive taste. Love? **(looking at Charlie tinkling away softly)** It does bring some happiness sometime, look at them, a few drinks, a few girls and they are all happy, how long though? Not long, because when it ends it can be hurtful, anyway, with some apologies I'll draw the line and let you get on with your beautiful piano... Oh, I forgot to tell you Charlie, it seems impossible that such a small word can create some many stories, perhaps including my own... but let's not dwell on things now, I wish I knew the answer, so for the moment let's drink to all the happy loves and sadly to my own sad love, on the other end I wish I could live on Champagne....

"Yes Joe, you could do that, but first let us do what we wrote when first the Tavern was opened..."

"Oh, yes Charlie.. I nearly forgot that... It was... `Just to live on Champagne` you haven't played that for a long time, do you remember it?"

"Of course I do Joe, just concentrate on he lyrics.....let's do it........ and one......two...three ...."

(Joe sings)

`Wouldn't it be nice/If I were a rich man/Wouldn't I think twice/Just to live on Champagne!/

"Wouldn't it be great/To be you at your own game/Would I hesitate?/Just to live on Champagne!/

`Oh that would be my life/Yes, no problems and no wife/Yes that would be my style/That would bring back my smile!

`I have paid the price/To be free of the pain/It would be so nice/Just to live on Champagne!

`Oh it is so nice....... Just to live on Champagne!!"

(It seems everyone's enjoying Charlie's instrumental as they all join in to the end, making the atmosphere jolly and happy and they also did appreciate Joe's lecture by the sound of their applause, even the girls applauded.)

"You see? **(looking at the crowd)** We could live wonderfully on Champagne, but it's only a dream for most of us, of course, love seems to be cheaper.... maybe....maybe... please hear me out....**(calling a chap from the crowd)** Hey you with the red hat...."

"Yes guv... what can I do for you?"

"Tell me, is your woman cheap or expensive?"

"Very cheap tonight, because I left her at home...ha,ha,ha!"

"Ha,ha,ha,ha, I like that mate.. Do you that all the time my friend?"

"Not always but I'll try my best, she won't let me, I've got to go easy otherwise she leaves me, but I think in the end I am glad to get home and find her there, because let's face it, we cannot live without them, our women will be always the number one in any families!! **(And raising his beer glass, likewise the crowd with big cheers)** I'll drink to that.. cheers to us all!" **(With Charlie playing the wedding march)**

Chapter 20

(It looks like his performance has given Joe a little hope of settling in with the crowd and of course with the girls)

"Poor old Joe, he tries very hard to make us believe he's happy. What do you think Lisa?"
"What do I think Lucy? I think he's only got himself to blame, and please don't say; poor old Joe, but silly old Joe!"
"**(Joe looking at the girls)** Did I hear my name mentioned by any chance....By the way Lucy... can you tell me a secret?"
(Lucy walks toward Joe and whispers)
"What secret do you want to know Joe?
"I know you know.... where Lisa stayed last night....sshhh, this is between you and me?"
"True... Nobody knows except me, she went back to her parents for good, that's what she said to me this morning!"
"You are lying Lucy, she couldn't have done that, because she left her purse at home, it's a long way to Leyton!"
"Ah.... did she?
"Yes she did......"
"Maybe she had some money in her bag....."
"She left her bag at home too....I take it you're a bit misinformed Lucy"
"Then she must have slept in a shop door way! Happy with my answer?"
"That's more like it Lucy..... my grateful thanks for being so kind, maybe one day you will tell me the real truth, I know you are the only one who knows it!"
"Perhaps I will, in the meantime we shall leave to that darling Joe!"
"Yes,This must be kept between you and me, that's what friends are for....Never forget that!"
"I won't Joe... you are so good planning your life....Ain't you?"
(And back she goes to the girls)
"Silly girl... I'm not planning it, I'm just taking it as it comes, and making the best of it, without the companionship of the female type!"
"Good for you Joe, you might not realize it..... but surely you are a lucky boy... or you were...."
"Thank you Lucy.......That's why they call me lucky Joe."
"Since when were you called lucky Joe?"
"Since the day I started to go out with a beautiful strange girl!"

"Don't think you're so lucky tonight Joe. I bet you can't tell me the name of that beautiful girl?"
"I don't think I can remember her name Lucy. But you are beautiful too Lucy.. is when I look into your eyes, your beauty tells me that I can't afford you!"
"I never knew I was so expensive, mind you in saying that, I could have been a bargain for you!"
"Good lord what a great mistake I must made, in spite of all, I still like you Lucy!"
(Lisa whisper to Lucy) "You can have him anytime Lucy... I know you are trying you best to make us speak... so I don't really care what you say to each other, it's not going to work, although I know he's not going to give in, he can be very selfish at times!"
"Well Lisa I tried my very best, sometimes you both behave like two little kids... no offense..."
"You might be right Lucy and to be honest it does reminds me the times we were in school, I just could not be too friendly with others, I think that's being a little upper class, and I don't think I am, anyway, that's in the past now... **(turning to Charlie)** Hi Charlie shall we do that blues we rehearsed this afternoon... I like that very much... and can you pass me the manuscript please?"
"You mean `You are my one and only` Here you are...."
"Can I have it in a minor key please?
"Of course my darling, no problems....... Here we are Lisa....... and... one, two...
(Lisa sings)
"You are my one and only/I love you, love you so/I feel ever so lonely/I wonder if you know!/
`You are my one and only/Please tell me what to do/I want you for me only/Just can't live without you! ---
`My life is yours, all yours/Please take it baby/Let me insist, oh yes/ Please don't say maybe!/
`You are my one and only/believe me it is true/I'm truly and immensely/So much in love with you!
`Let us be together/And in love forever........."
(The girls were the first standing up and clapping, followed by all the others)
"Well done Lisa, considering it's your first time since you rehearsed it this afternoon!"

"Many thanks Lucy, I tried my best, don't forget you'll have to learn this yourself too!"
"I will don't worry, because I like it very much. I could see that you sung it with more feeling than any other song, was it for someone in particular, there again I could be wrong!"
"Oh I don't know Lucy, it's only a song, then again it seems to be tailored for a lost love and if you meant that, you could be right! But you might sing it to one of your pretenders in future!"
"That's a good idea, but I'll have to find one first. Oh.... I promise I shall not make any more comments on the subject, we have a long evening to go, and I don't really want you to go home again in tears **(and softly)** You probably noticed that he's been making enquiries, regarding your evacuation last night, I'm afraid to say that you forgot your purse which it's still in your bag at your place, he thinks you couldn't have possibly gone back to your parents without any money. Anyway, you are staying with me tonight. Are you?"
"Yes I do Lucy and I appreciate that very much! Thank you for the key."
"You won't need it tonight, as we shall be walking home together....I don't want any more male bodyguard, **(and softly)** like last night! I say Lisa.... we haven't seen our friend yet... I heard John telling Joe, that he was up stairs in the office!"
"Please leave him there....... Oh, oh... there he is.... I can see him talking to Don....Don't laugh Lisa, look at his black eye..."
"Please don't make me laugh Lucy, we don't want people to find out..."
"Say no more Lisa....subject closed!"
(Joe's drowning his sorrows with a second pint of good Ale, but, by the look on his face, he seems feeling very sorry for himself, suspecting that lovey-dovey song was probably dedicated to him, sadly, what can he do? nothing really, unless some good ideas will spring up to his mind.... suddenly he looks up and sees Bertie looking at him with a grin on his face)
"What you smiling at Bertie, do I look like a clown?"
"Sorry Joe, I'm simply smiling because... you look as though... well... it seems that the world has crushed on you, you should be a happy man mate.... Have you seen the new record of your love? At least you have a famous member in the family now..."
"I am not really bothered about the record, anyway, I haven't got a gramophone, so it is no use to me, and as for a famous member in the family, I would correct that...ex family you mean....!"

"Come on Joe, you are exaggerating now, mind you look as though you lost a million dollars!"
"Yeah... You are wrong I lost a diamond, a diamond that walks, in fact if you want to know... that diamond just walked out on me! I thought I would never have had the courage to say that.....Does it satisfy you?"
"Not really, I don't like to see you like that, you are my best mate, and we must support each other, no matter the problems."
"You are right Bertie, I really do appreciate your concern, but a little bird told me that you lost your diamond too, was it because you didn't look after your diamond properly?"
"Right you are Joe, I lost my diamond too, it's ironically really, you lost your diamond here in the Tavern, and lost my diamond in the Market, we tried to patch it up, but you know with my Rosie you just can't win with her, why she done it, I can't really explain it... but I am happy!"
"Yes I was witnessing some kind of bickering earlier on, in the Market, but as you say you are happy, and that is the main thing in life! I do envy you Bertie.... lucky fellow."
"Yes I'm happy and in good health too, I do think it's not the end of the world, it was only a little argument, she made a drama out of it....but she'll come around sooner or later!"
"I'm not criticizing you Bertie we all have arguments! And talking about good health or physical fitness, can you tell me what happened to your eye...?. Was that a reply from Rosie? Now I know the reason why you were wearing dark glasses this afternoon!"
"Ain't it marvellous......Everyone thinks that Rosie gave me this black eye, I'm getting annoyed with that, it was not Rosie, I had an accident in the cellar this afternoon a bottle fell on me from the top shelf, and as for wearing my glasses this afternoon I just felt like wearing glasses.. because my eyes needed relaxing a bit..... with this lighting in here, they do feel hitching now and then, and because of the accident Don told me I could have the evening off, so we called in John!"
"Evening off for a black eye? That man spoils you rotten, you have all the luck, believe me!"
"Well, I was going to take the evening off anyway, as I might keep Rosie company when she comes in! In fact Don suggested that, as I have been working very hard lately!"
"Oh yes? Please tell me another.... I saw John earlier, good old John, he slaves all day long and then to make ends meet he comes here to give you some leisurely life... so who's the lucky fellow that made you a fool then, don't tell me is one of our good friends?"

"You never going to believe this, is that old Greasy but I haven't got any proofs, I always knew he fancied her, but there again..it's always ends like that, the victim is the last to know....Call him a good friend, Yeack!"

"Ah,ah,ah, Oh, forgive me to laugh Bertie, do you really think that Rosie would waste her time with Greasy? With all great respect I've got for Greasy, you are soooo wrong!"

"You never know my friend, anything can happen now days, **(very softly)** You know women can be very fussy.... they want to experiment anything, from the good, the bad and the ugly, as long they enjoy it... say no more!" **(touching his nose with his thumb)**

"Would you mind telling me which category you belong to? As for myself I would classify myself as normal.... but you, alright you think you are God's gift to women, don't be offended by my remark, and you always think you can get what you want, remember the grass is not always greener on the other side!"

"Okay Joe, the fact is that it's not a laughing matter, at least your Lisa, didn't go with someone else.....unfortunately!"

"Unfortunately. What do mean by that Bertie, did you think Lisa would go with someone else?"

"NO....nooooo, would I think of that about Lisa? It's just a way of saying!"

"Way of saying? I don't really get that Bertie, you know damn well that my Lisa wouldn't do that!"

"Yes of course not, but as I said before, women can be very fussy. And may I remind you that she's not your Lisa anymore until she comes back to you, and secondly you sound as if you are jealous!"

"There you go again, How many times do I have to tell you that I am not jealous Bertie, I have a hunch that you might know more than I do, don't forget that I work all day long, I only see her in the evening and you patronise our territory almost all day, watching them skirts walking up and down! It must be a nice hobby for you, on the other hand you were made for that!"

"There's no need to get so worked up Joe, we can't be all the same, quite simply during the day I plan my work for the evening! and watching the girls go by it helps me to concentrate on my job!"

"Oh yes... You are planning your work for the evening, by watching the girls go by... Eh? Have you ever thought that Rosie might get lonely sometimes, with all respects!"

Chapter 21

(Charlie was listening with interest their silly conversation, plus that wasn't a miss to the girls too)

"I never enjoyed myself so much listening to you two, perhaps I am not the only one, look at the sweethearts!"
"We don't take any notice of you lot, but you are welcome to listen as this is grown up talks and you might learn something!"
"Did you hear that Charlie? I must say this is my friend preacher talking!"
"I am listening Joe.... I'm enjoying my break, couldn't be better!"
"Are you with me Joe or with Charlie? Alright, maybe I have neglected her a bit, but this is not unusual after such a long time of marital union, I'd like to see you Joe, after a few years of marriage... that is if you ever get married!"
(Joe's looking at Charlie again) "Do I really have to listen to this kind of preaching.. **(and turning to Bertie)** Mr Valentino or Don Juan if you prefer!
(The discussion becomes so hot that the girls cannot avoid listening.)
"How about that Lisa, they're rather amusing, no need to question them, we hear all the answers!"
"You are right Lucy, they probably don't realize what they say.... it's quite a good show, listen..!"
"Anyway Joe, I hope you are not sulking now!"
"No.. it's alright Bertie, I have come to the conclusion that I can take anything now....I just give up."
"I was exaggerating when I moaned about my marriage, so I will correct myself.....Let me tell you that Rosie and I are still consuming our home made honey, if you know what I mean, although is good to have a little argument now and then as it helps us to live together happily!"
"What in blue blazers are you talking about?"
"Okay let's drink to that then... no more talking about the girls, but one more question: How many girls have you had Joe?"
"No more questions? Now, You're getting a bit personal now Bertie, what difference does it makes, how many girls anyone's had? Sometimes it's not the quantity but the quality of just one!"
"You know my brother keeps bragging about how many girls he's had!"
"Your rascal brother talks too much!"
"I know mate, he even tried to stir up troubles between me and Rosie!"

(**Joe whisper to the crowd)** That's a laugh, I don't know who's the biggest liar of the two.. (**And turning to Bertie)** What troubles? I thought that you and Rosie had only a little arguments!"

"Oh I don't know Joe, do you think we live in a crappy old world?

"No Bertie, our world is nice, maybe you should think at the times when you were selling houses, that was probably a crappy world for you, and now look at you, you are in charge of all this, you couldn't be a luckier fellow...."(**Charlie tinkles away the old song "Oh What a World" softly)**

"Never mind what you think friend......"Oh, what a world Joe, everyone's going crazy, we lost our girls, and we become so lazy...."

"Oh, what a world Bertie, you might speak the truth my friend, we lost our girls, we don't remember when!"

"Let me give you some advice Bertie mate, if you want peace you just gotta wait!"

"Okay my good friend Joe, something 's got to happen now, if not we'll manage somehow!"

"Oh what a world Bertie we don't really deserve this......

"Too true Joe, what we want is only peace....... Just peace with a kiss...!"

(**Charlie ends it with glissando)**

"Thank you Charlie, I liked your gentle backing with a tumbling at the end. You know Bertie the more I look at your black eye, the more I think of Rosie, what's the truth then, come on be fair!"

"NO... she did not punch me, further more she wouldn't dare to lay a finger on me, no woman has laid a finger on me so far, and for the second time it was bottle that fell on me in the cellar.

"Poor old Bertie, something tells me that you are lying, but as you are my good friend I am incline to believe you, for this I am offering you my sincere sympathy and for this I will buy you another drink, it'll do you good to your eye!"

"Don't tell me you feel sorry for me!"

"I only feel sorry for you because by losing one eye you could have lost half of the number of girls that usually you eye up and down....ha,ha,ha,"

"You are so funny, you should be on stage, and think you are exaggerating Joe, I resent that, after all we've been friends for years!"

"Alright Bertie, I'm sorry about your eye, but fancy loosing Rosie!"

"I haven't lost her as such, but what she's done she need a kick up her....."

"Hold on Bertie there's no need to be hasty, or nasty, let us be civilised!"

"Okay Joe, maybe deep down I'm a little upset! What about you? What made you react the way you did, just for a silly quarrel? I think that was really a childish mistake Joe!"

"It wasn't for the quarrel we had in here Bertie, the big one was at home last night when she kept telling me, that I was wrong to behave as I did in the Tavern, okay, I might have gone over the top, but accusing me of being jealous.... no...oh...no... well that infuriated me!"

"Come of it Joe, you are a bit jealous, sorry let me refrain that... you are bloody jealous!"

"Don't you start, and there's no need to swear, she really drove me to the point to tell her that I didn't love her anymore!"

"Well... (**whispering)** that sums up the truth then, she must have had a good reason to packs her bags and stay with someone else!"

"Hold on...Hold on...mate! How do you know she packed her bags and stay with someone else? I suppose you were there too.....Eh?"

"Come on don't be silly Joe **(tapping his nose with his finger)** everyone knows what happened, remember we have the local newscaster keeping us up to date, have you tried to rescue her yet? Pull yourself together man, I bet she's waiting for you to make the first move."

"You must be joking, I certainly will not make the first move, I like to see you doing that with Rosie, when she'll arrive, that is IF she'll come....!"

"Quite honestly I wouldn't Joe, because my situation is much worse than yours, and of course she will come here tonight, because she knows that our marriage is in peril, and the first consideration is the marriage, which makes more difficult to split up.... then I've got some pride you know... being made a fool is terrible!"

"Don't make me laugh Bertie, you don't know the meaning of that word!"

"Well let me tell my good friend (**Whispering)** my problem is there.... sitting at the bar, my so called friend Greasy''' hush...hush.. "(**zipping his lips**)

"This has made my evening complete Bertie, I promise I won't laugh, even if I want to, I don't want to offend you! Greasy.... Greasy.... as I said before..... don't make me laugh!"

"Please don't do me any favours Joe, Greasy is not different than you or me, apart to say that he's not very good looking and well educated like you and me, but let us not forget that he's a man!"

"Yes Bertie, but I cannot believe that Rosie would waste her time with Greasy, how many times do I have to tell you this?."

"Perhaps you are right Joe and I thank you for being serious for a change, but women are very particular in fancying the opposite sex, for example; I used to know a beauty six foot tall that she ended up in bed with a midget four foot six man!"
"Lucky midget..... Who's that six foot beauty then Bertie?"
"That's not funny Joe, anyway, I think I've got a suggestion..."
"Oh yeah...? Spit it out then.... it better be good"
"First of all we are the superior species, and quite frankly we are more clever that the female ones."
"That might be true, but they still do what they want Bertie."
"Like the hell they do, I think it's about time we collect our properties, and this is my plan... just listen carefully... **(in saying that Rosie appears behind Bertie's back)**
"Are you referring me as your property by any chance? I know you used to be a property's agent long ago, does this mean that you can treat me like some kind of property? And what is your plan?"
"Talk of the devil in disguise... I seem to know that sweet voice...(**and turning around**)... Ah..it's you Rosie.. I thought I was dreaming for a moment... Good Gawd, I would never think that you are my property....NO WAY....But let me say, with your permission... that...that you must be a magician to appear just like that... (**Clicking his fingers)** are you real? The alcohol must have given me abbreviations!"
"You mean hallucinations you twerp... and of course I'm real!"
Ah.. you must think that I cannot speak properly, but I do remember your little escapades with that mate of mine!"
"Say what you like Bertie make it a priority if you like, now I'm busy... go back to your dreams!"
"Okay, okay, there's no need to be nasty sweetheart!"
"That's only the beginning the rest will follow... and don't sweetheart me, get your act together man!"
"But Rosie.... just listen... don't be so complicated...."
"Complicated?? I haven't got time to listen to your rubbish.... just sober up, look at you a couple of pints and you are falling on the floor!"
"See what I mean Joe? With a woman like mine you never can win, no matter what you say. Have I not tried? Yes I did!"
"Please Bertie, be quite for one second, let us seriously think a way out!"
"If you say so Joe... I feel a little bit down in the dumps.... so to speak!"
"Come on then Bertie pull yourself up, get rid of that pride, even if you don't see eye to eye!"

"That's not funny Joe, one more remark like that and I will wear my dark glasses again!"
"Now then Bertie, be serious, sometimes we must succumb, no matter the situation!"

(As the girls are having their short break, Rosie joins them for a little chat.)
"Hello girls may I join you?"
"Of course Rosie, take a seat, we are rather enjoying this."
"We heard you giving your Bertie a telling off, I don't think he expected that in front of his mate!"
"You probably right Lucy, but now and then it's good to remind him who's the boss!"
"Well I would have done the same if I had a husband or a boyfriend...**(Looking at Lisa)**
"Just look at them Lisa, can't believe the state they are in, are they real? Am I really married to one of them?"
"Oh.... don't worry too much Rosie, let them roast, they might come to their senses soon!"
"Nice of you to say so Lisa, but one thing that baffles me, no one seems to be able to give me a good answer about Bertie's black eye, I thought it was a bit odd to see him wearing dark glasses in the Market, funny I didn't realized it at home, maybe because we are not on full speaking terms, actually if I said anything he turned his face!"
"Are you really in bad terms Rosie, have you asked Don?"
"Yes we asked him Lucy, however, Don says that he had an accident in the cellar, so he gave him a night off... you know what he said? The poor man...... can't work in them conditions.... I just couldn't believe it, that man spoils him rotten, he treats him like a son sometimes, I am not complaining about that, taking in consideration that he' a damn good worker and loyal, anyway, do you know anything about his eye then?" **(Rosie's asking the girls)**
"Well... we know as much as you do, and don't take it too hard, in a couple of days he'll be back to normal, fit as anything to give us his usual charm..." **(the girls burst out laughing)**
"That's what worries me, when he's back with his usual charm....It's easy for you to laugh, I know it sounds funny, but I've got to live with him, that is if we are not going to split up, according to the actual situation!"
"Come on Rosie your situation is not all that serious!"

"Thank you Lisa, but when you are married the situation is more serious, and getting more difficult to separate!"

"Now, now then Rosie, I think you are exaggerating a little bit, you are not the only one who have problems, you know?"

"Yes I know Lisa, no one is perfect, as for exaggerating I could be, but when I'm being accused of having had an affair... which is not true, let alone anything else, I don't find it very funny!"

"Well then, in that case you have nothing to worry about!"

"Many thanks Lisa, for your reassurance **(and whispering)** Between you lot and the four walls, I still love the old rascal...**(turning to Lisa)** how about you Lisa... let us have the truth, as we all know that you have a little problem too..... do you still love him?"

"Yes... unfortunately my heart says yes, but....he must control his possessiveness or jealousy! "

"Maybe you are right Lisa, sometimes we have to throw away that stupid pride, so for the moment let us have a good laugh......."

Chapter 22

(Two well dressed young men enter the Tavern, and approach the girls table.

"Good evening ladies, may we introduces ourselves? I am William, Will to my friends, and this is my good friend and partner Gary, we don't mean to intrude... may we join you? We are two lucky chaps who won a considerable sum of money at the races today, if you don't mind we would like you all to share with us a few bottles of bubbly! Don't worry this is a straight friendly offer!"

Well... it is our short break, we don't really mind, it's nice to share some wealth, as we certainly cannot afford such luxury! Then consider yourselves welcome to our table.... "

That's it then.... Gary please go an order three bottles of the best Champagne, nice and chilled!"

"Okay Will, I will settle as well....Is that okay?"

"You do as you think best... the money comes out from one wallet only... hurry up I am thirsty.... **(looking at Rosie)** And what's your name darling..."

"Rosie... then we have Lisa...Lucy...Jane.. Viv and Gina... there's another one she's maybe indisposed.... "

"You are all lovely and so are your names, it's nice to meet you all!"

"You are new around here, as we've never seen you before!"

"That's alright Rosie, we work in the city, we are stockbrokers...!"

"Stockbrokers? Are you the ones who break up the banks?"

"No sweetheart, we are stock brokers, not stock breakers, we don't break the banks..a totally different profession."

"I'm only joking mate, I know exactly what brokers do, in fact, my first boyfriend was a broker, he liked money so much that he ended up himself broke...ha,ha,hha,ha,.."

"That's good Rosie, you never told us that!"

"Well there are a lot of things that I never divulge to my friends, neither to ex husband!"

"So you are divorce then Rosie....Please tell us more!

"Just thinking, just thinking William..."

"Well It's your lucky day, I think you just found a lucky contender"

"Thank you but I think I am not ready neither available as yet...!"

"Oh I see you have a new record released..... you must be well know in the music business then."

"It is our first, and they are for sale, and for you we will also sign it....
"OOOH that's nice we shall have a few of them.... are you then the main singer Lisa?... "
"Yes I am.. but Charlie over there is the greatest...He can make his piano talk, you know what I mean?"
"Got you! Thank you very much... we have so many music lovers, it'll be a nice present for them!"
"How many do you want? I shall have them packed for you!"
"I think we'll have six.. thank you! Oh here we are then, let us drink to your good health, and to your lucky future Rosie!
"Oh thank you Will, and thanks Gary.. let's drink to your good luck.....
"And... Lucy are you married then?"
"No she's not married."
"Thank you Rosie, I should have said that..."
"Sorry darling you've got to be quick with some men, before they change their mind."
"Don't worry Rosie, you are quite right, I suppose as a married woman you know more than us singles!"
"You are probably right you too Lucy, but to be honest I've learned that after I got married, to be very careful of single girls, they seem to have a taste for married men, please forgive me this is not a criticism on yourself but on the entire single generation!"
"Well..well, we are all singles here and you are a very suspicious wife, it gives me an impression that you don't trust your husband, I always thought that marriage is made up of trust!"
"Yes Indeed, is made up to a certain point Lucy...."
"I must admit Rosie, that I'm glad to say, that I've never ever thought to have an affair with a married man... ain't that true Lisa?
"True Lucy, but I wonder what it's like to have one....."
"I couldn't tell you Lisa, as I have never had one. You must confide in everything you two, but I'm proud of you Lucy, because if I ever knew that my Bertie had an affair with a single woman I would certainly feed him to the rats and skin her alive!"
Goodness me Rosie you are ferocious!"
"No I did not mean that.... I would kill him first....ha,ha,ha,ha,ha!"
"I must say you are some girl Rosie... I could do with you in my office to get the rest of my staff in line, you can have a job if you like, I will pay you well, as you'd be the manageress!"
"Thank you for the offer William, but I've got a job already, actually two jobs!"

"Two jobs.... goodness me you are busy....That's a pity, I could do with one like you, you've got the power I require. Gary I think they are all taken and very busy these beautiful girls, so we better forget to be contenders, never mind we are here to enjoy a glass of bubbly!"
"And nice it is too, we are being spoiled, a very good health to all of us!"

"Hey Joe, just listen to Rosie, she really can get into any conversation, and she knows how to put the men where they belong to, **(and shouting across)** Hi Rosie are they bothering you them two aliens?"
"Who's that fellow.....? Why is he shouting at us..?"
"Don't worry Gary leave that fellow to me.... Hey you two sleeping beauties, funny you mention that, I wonder who's the aliens now, and without spaceship... so zip up!"
"Well said young lady.."
"You know William I always wanted to be a police woman, then of course I didn't like the way the policemen behave, so I gave up the idea!"
"Goodness me Rosie, you seem to have an answer for everything!"
"That's life Lucy!"
"Drink up girls if it's not enough we shall order another bottle!"
"Don't worry Will I've already left a couple of bottles in the wood for these girls, as they have been very nice and good company!"
"Goodness me you two you certainly live in another world, you lucky devils!"
"We earn good money, and why not spend it!"
"Did you hear that girls? That's the way the other half lives!" **(The girls smile at the them lifting up their glasses for a happy cheer)**

(Looks like Bertie and Joe are looking down at their empty glasses, and it seems they even run out of conversation.)
"Well I can see your neighbours haven't said anything for quite a while, perhaps they are no longer interested in what we think a beautiful bunch of roses, meaning you girls, and what a remarkable place this is, I just love the atmosphere, we'll certainly be back again I can promise you, come to think of it I seem to remember reading the name "The Piccadilly Tavern" somewhere!"
"You are right Will, some friends of our mention it the last Gazette!"
"Thank you William.. and thank you Gary for your compliments and the exquisite company which was quite unexpected, not to mention the

pleasant bubbly... but unfortunately it's time we say good bye as the girls they got to go back on the stage!"
"That's no problems Lisa, in fact we were just about leaving.... I just remember...Gary for goodness sake we are late to meet those people at the Savoy Hotel!"
"Don' t forget your records William, they are all packed, you can settle for them at the counter!"
"Oh thank you Rosie... I'll do that right away....
"Come on Will... I'll wait outside we might need a taxi, hope we can find one....Goodbye girls!"
"Goodbye everyone......
(And out they went happily)
"That's it girls we nearly got rid of fifty records!"
"That's wonderful Lisa....."
"Never mind girls, I've got an idea, we have two bottle of bubbly in the wood, and that money we can use it to pay for a record each, actually there's even enough for a record for you Rosie!"
"Good idea and thank you... now I shall have to buy a gramophone as we don't have one....."
"Bertie did say he'd like to buy you one.... you heard him too Lisa, didn't you?"
"Yes I heard him, I do remember it well Rosie, he told us when we arrived earlier on!"
"You two girls seem to know about my husband more than I do, he never said anything to me about the gramophone, very strange!"
"Maybe he wanted to surprise you, you know what he's like with girls!"
"Yes Rosie, he mentioned that when the records were delivered, please ask him..!"
"I will, don't you worry about that, I've got so many bones to pick with him, you have no idea!"

Chapter 23

(Between the sound of the music and the people Joe and Bertie are still planning their rescue)

"I suppose they didn't know my Rosie. Eh.. Joe? What a girl, she certainly knows how to handle men and their money!"

"You must really love her in spite of your bragging.... Please tell me; does she handles you like that when it come to money, I know you are very mean when it comes to spending it!"

"You could be right Joe... and don't forget I pay the bills...hey.... they must have been really loaded. Did you see the girls expressions when they said they had to meet someone at the Savoy Hotel? What's more to buy six records, they must have been out of their mind!"

"Yuck... don't believe everything you see or hear Bertie, first of all anyone can buy six records, I wouldn't take much notice of their conversation, maybe they were just showing off!"

"However, I don't think they were interested in any of the girls, except that William offered a job to my Rosie, she knew how to put him in his place, I don't think Rosie is very fond of that high class lot, she's really deep down a plain East ender!"

"Yes Bertie... that shows you that the grass is not always greener on the other side!"

"Good point Joe, listen to this: **(shouting to the girls)** Hey girls, congratulations, maybe they were too good for you... plenty dosh, good looking young men.... Bachelors .... shame really!"

"We are not desperate like you, **(looking at Bertie)** we don't need something on the side to keep us going, and we don't look around for love affairs.... with single girls!"

"love affairs Lucy...With single girls.... Has he been up to something that I don't know about?"

"No Rosie, I just said it to make him wonder, why I said it I simply don' know, and you should know that they are all talk and no do!"

"Not if they get a chance, especially my one Lucy.... I tell you he would fulfil his ambitions... with all his credentials!"

"Did you hear that Joe? Love affairs...... **(looking at Rosie)** let me remind someone about her love affair, hicks, with one of my supposed friend... I tell you what... I believe, not only guess that love affair was a flop... floppy.. floppy...floppy and crappy love affair... hick..hick.... I think that was funny Joe... very funny!"

"No, I don't think that was funny at all Bertie, you are only making the situation worse than it is, that is affecting ME! First of all, I never had any love affairs at all, so they are out of my list, secondly, I don't want to take part of these kind of talks, so no more comments on that subject please, I only wish Don kept you on duty tonight, you wouldn't have said stupid things!"
"Oh.. you are getting touchy mate, I was talking good sense if you don't mind!"
"That might be so, but now we have our spectators starting to take some notice of our silly conversations and comments, which I think they are rubbish."
"Yes Joe we can hear you both, especially you Bertie loud and clear, why not try to behave in a civilized manner?"
"Why do I get the blame all the time, I simply don't know... Okay my darling Rose....
"And don't darling me, look at the state of you, any girl that sees you, would certainly run a mile, mind you, she'll probably do you a favour. "
"What kind of flavour, my sweet flossy...!
"It's favour, not flavour and don't flossy me... never mind.... OH......Men.....MEN...!"

(The girls go back to their stage for some more dancing, while Lisa's looking through the manuscript book for her next song. Rosie's about to leave, but Lisa asks her to stay a little longer.)
"Thank goodness we are on our own Rosie, I've got something to tell you, I was going to leave it until later, but I just can't wait!"
"Good Lord Lisa, that sounds important, go on, don't keep me in suspense, I'm getting as bad as Nosey Pete!"
"Well, a few weeks ago I was approached by a distinguished gentleman here in the Tavern, and to cut a long story short, he turn out to be the staff director of the cruise company "The Blue Seas" he offered me a top job for a world cruise, he told me most of the details, such as; this cruise will last more than three months, naturally all this will be on my contract, it was very tempting on my side, we met in a cafe' the next day for further details, at first I was a bit suspicious, although he showed me his credentials and he gave me some beautiful brochures, but then when he suggested that contracts would be signed at his offices here in London. I told him I was interested provided he would let me take my make up girl, without hesitation he said yes.. I thought of

you Rosie, if you are interested you'll have to sign the contract like myself, this will have to be done in a couple of weeks time, that will give me enough time to get acquainted with the musicians I will work with!"
"I am flabbergasted Lisa... I am very tempted, I think I might accept the offer, after all what's new around here? Day in, day out, it's quite a boring routine and I'll be honest with you, we'll no longer put up twenty four hours a day with them two rascals, least of all we are going to see how the other half lives, I guess it'll be just like a holiday!"
"True Rosie, but let us not build up too many dreams, we got quite a few bridges to cross, on the safe side give it another thought, I don't want you to think that I'm pushing you too much into it!"
"Never mind about that Lisa... I just can't wait, I bet we'll meet some nice fellows on board!"
"You bet we will Rosie, and fellows with lots of dosh, not like some, penniless we know!"

(Although Bertie and Joe were in complete silence, but not completely in another world, Bertie manages to catch some of their discussion.)
"Are you talking about us Lisa... we got plenty money too... you know?"
"Plenty money...yuck...more likely plenty lice, look at him Lisa, is just about to scratch his head!"
"Rosie why are you so nasty, he doesn't do you any harm at all?"
"Well, for a start you should not be so nosey Bertie, and secondly you should not interfere. See... what I have to put up with... Day in day out??"
"Don't take any notice Rosie, as I was saying; the other thing is that I've already given a month notice to Don, I explained to him about the new job, he wished me good luck, but he said that it wasn't the kind of news he really wanted to hear on his birthday, and on the first anniversary of the Tavern, I felt so bad about it, but I just could not go back on my words, perhaps I should have waited until tomorrow! Then he asked me, if that was anything to do with the quarrel I had with Joe, I said not at all, This offer came a couple of weeks ago, strangely enough I never told Joe, as I wasn't sure I was taking it or not, I thought it was simply about my career!"
"I understand you Lisa, I know you couldn't help it, and of course, you probably feel a little bit guilty because the Tavern gave you the first

break, and then....I'm sure Joe will get over it!"

(Lucy come along)

"Hi Lisa, what's this about your new Job? Don was telling me that you gave a month notice! Is that the secret you were going to tell me?"

"Yes, I was going to tell you Lucy and I even thought of offering you to come with me, but I thought it wouldn't have been fair to take away staff from the Tavern, it's bad enough me leaving."

"Very thoughtful of you Lisa, but I would have had to decline, however, it was nice of you to think of me, but the Tavern is okay by me, beside I've got my mum to look after, as you know she still lives on her own most of the times, she's been wonderful to me!"

"But I'm sure it'll be terrific opportunity for you Lucy... with your figure and your skills."

"No Rosie, thank you for your compliments, truth is that if the chance comes along, I'd rather settle around here!"

(**Bertie hears Lucy's comment)**"Fine chance that will be...... not if you go around punching innocent people!"

"What's he talking about Lucy?"

"Oh... nothing Rosie, Bertie means the little incident that occurred the other evening in the Tavern, I slapped someone because he touched my leg, poor fellow he really didn't mean it, he did apologize in the end, mind you I didn't hurt him at all, it was just a gentle slap, I suppose it would have been worse if I had punched him in his eye, but I was kind enough not to do that!"

"See what I mean Lucy? You only have to smile at them and they think they own you....men, men!"

"You are so right Rosie... but that is the men mentality!"

(Bertie replies) "Sorry about my remark Lucy, I forgot about that slapping, I'm losing my memory!"

"Don't worry Bertie, I know how you feel.... of.. having the responsibility in keeping the Tavern quite and clean from nasty fellows, still, so far our customers seem to behave alright!"

(Meanwhile Nosey Pete is having a quite drink with his friends)

"You know Greasy, I think you should take it a little easier, you seem to have too many commitments now days, let your cousin Fred managed the stall!"

"You must be joking Pete, he'll go bankrupt in no time, he hasn't got any brains at all, all he can do properly is to pull the cart!"

"I wouldn't have thought that, he seems to be quite clever when he talks and very polite to his customers, in fact I was impressed yesterday when he sold them two old candelabras "

"Oh yes? He sold them two candelabras for half of the price stated, just because the buyer bargained so much, he got confused and let them go at the buyer's price!"

"Well... stone me... I am surprised... that's not very good for business Greasy, I bet you were annoyed!"

"That's not everything my boy, for instance the other day he was selling staff for peanuts, he got mixed up between shillings and pennies, for a moment I really thought he could not read the price, mind you between us, he was very bad at school, he couldn't add up at all!"

"That's not good... is it? You might as well put your wife in charge, she's quite good."

"Oh yes? It's like going out of the pan into the fire, she's bloody worse, if you know what I mean."

"Yeah I know exactly what you mean Greasy, still you can't have everything perfect in life, we all have our ups and down, and so is my bruv I do try my best to tell him the right things he just won't listen!"

"Yeah... what a family I have....Pete and you know what? They cost me a fortune, I only wish I married a woman like your sister in law... yeah... she's a clever lass... your brother is very lucky and sometimes he doesn't appreciate it, but I must say he's good at his job here in the Tavern!"

"Yes Rosie is a clever girl, she knows how to run the budget in the house, I tell you something Greasy, you don't see a lot of waste going into the rubbish bin, and she knows how to keep an eye on him.... mind you if must know he's always keeping an eye on her, my bruv is quite possessive and jealous, I can't imagine what it would do if she goes with another fellow, so I warn you!"

"ME? I even wouldn't dare to look at her.. plus we know that, in fact by keeping an eye on her so much he nearly lost one, please don't you go and tell him, he'll do his nut..... Did she do it?

"Ah! The story of his eye.. I don't think so Greasy, Rosie wants to know how it happened, and I have been trying to find out the real truth, although it seems to me that the story of the bottle, doesn't square up, on the other hand, if the bottle fell from the top shelf, it might have caused the accident, I will investigate if he takes me down in that cellar, mind you.... it could have been worse!"

"Silly bagger... Here comes Stanley, you wanted to ask him something.... didn't you?"

"Oh yes... Hi Stanley.... I know what I meant to ask you....Why the ol' Bill never checked your goods this morning? At the time I didn't take much notice, but as I was having my dinner, I was talking to Rosie about it, she asked me if the PC plod checked everyone, I thought for a moment, and I realized that he forgot you. Are you related to him by any chance?"

"You must be joking, would I be related to a copper, if I was I wouldn't be certainly have a stall in England, I'd probably emigrate to Australia...ha,ha,ha, Maybe he was thinking about your salty tea!"

"Your are so funny Stanley.... you jammy sod, you have all the luck in the world, we all know that underneath your stall you kept some secret goods...ha,ha,ha,ha!

"Please don't tell anyone, and keep your voice down.....you never know who's next to us.. we don't want another visit from our friendly pod, then we could be really in trouble...ha,ha,ha,ha!"

"That's the way to be..... one for all....all for one...ha,ha,ha..........crafty old sod......"

Chapter 24

(Louise and Bob just arrived from the Savoy Theatre)

"Hello Louise, hello Bob, how was the show then?"
"Hi Don, that was really wonderful, the music, the lyrics and the atmosphere was simply astonishing, and the Theatre was completely full, what a performance and the music was superb!"
"what was it called?"
"`Young Lovers` an intrigue love story of two young lovers, with the extraordinary problems of their families, not in accordance with the lovers situation, actually the girl's parents wanted an arranged marriage with someone else, quite fascinating really! I think you ought to go and see it Don, you will enjoy it!"
"Of course I might do that, but something like that still happens now days in some eastern Countries!"
"Oh, it was sad and funny sometimes..Don, but with an happy ending. Talking about young lovers, have they made it up yet?"
"No Louise, they still don't talk."
"Incidentally Don, I met young Lisa in the Market this morning, I congratulated her for singing and then I met the young man in question as I needed some groceries, don't worry I was very discrete with both of them. I know they are both nice and I wouldn't interfere in their relation, because it has nothing to do with me, shame really, they are such a lovely couple!"
"Too right Louise, it's nothing to do with me neither... it's their problem and it doesn't concern us whatsoever, and as for Lisa... Well...she's leaving the Tavern, for a better job, she has given me a month notice... really, that wasn't the kind of present I really wanted on my birthday and on my Tavern first anniversary... I really think the world of her, but there you are, facts of life I suppose!"
"Happy birthday my dear Don, what a lovely surprise, on the Tavern anniversary.. No.. I won't ask your age, but you will allow me to buy a bottle of your best bubbly, and as for Lisa.... what can I say? I know she's a great asset to you, but there's simply nothing you can do, if only I could put a few words in on your behalf, but I don't really know her that well, and of course it's her choice!"

"It is her choice indeed Louise, and neither of us can do anything about it, in this case I shall go and order the bottle of bubbly!"
"Make sure the best one you deserve it.....
(Bob tries to correct Louise feelings whilst Don goes to the bar)
"Louise darling, maybe I think you should control your feelings what doesn't concern you"
"You are so right Bob, I am sorry it was very immature of me, but I feel so sorry for Don, is such a wonderful employer, and I thought he doesn't deserve lo lose that lovely singer!"
Few minutes later the Champagne is brought over by Don himself
"Thank you Don I think you should have had the waitress to bring it, especially on your birthday!"
"To be honest darling I like a bit of exercise, and today is my chance, as my good Bertie has the evening off and John his replacement is very busy with other customers!"
"that's alright, he's sitting over there with... what's his name....?"
"Joe, Bertie keeps him company, after that small accident in the cellar, don't laugh a bottle fell on him from the top shelf and gave him a black eye...... the funny thing is that everyone thinks his wife gave him the black eye, you really got to laugh sometimes.......What do you know!?"
"Ah,ah,ah,ah....that is most peculiar, and hard to believe Don, however I find it very unfortunate.. by the way, is Bertie's wife here tonight?"
"Oh yes Louise, there she is talking to Lisa!"
"Oh...I say.. she's very attractive you were right... well...... What a good looking girl, I think they make a very nice couple!"
"Not only that but she's very jealous of him, if I may say so!"
"If she's jealous it means she loves him very much...Don!"
"I think she does, but Bertie has eyes for a lot of girls, sorry let me refrain that, tonight he has only one eye.... and at the moment he's a bit cheerful as he's had a few pints, I don't mind it is its evening off, as when he's on duty he doesn't touch a drop!"
"I like your sense of humour Don, and you must appreciate that on duty he's very strait. It's nice to have a head barman with responsibility. Anyway let us have a toast to your birthday Don, am I exaggerating if I say; to the next fifty?
"You are being too generous Louise, maybe I could accept another forty!"
"Likewise for you Bob?"
"Thank you, you are so kind Louise. Incidentally, I noticed that you sale

records too. Was that stand there last night?"

"Well...... not really, the story goes that a few months ago we were lucky enough to have a visit from Radio Mercury, they recorded live two songs, and I thought to contact Singalong record company, they liked them, and subsequently I came up with the idea to have them published and released them on record on the day of the anniversary, we already sold quite a few copies here tonight, but from tomorrow they will be on sale all over England!"

"Was Radio Mercury kind enough, to let the record company to use the recording?

"Not so easy, we came to an agreement, and there are a few people involve, but mainly it is good for us, also because the songs were written.. one by Charlie the piano player and Bertie, and the other by Joe and Lisa!"

"Very clever lot you've got here..."

"Thank you Bob... they are very good. They are kind, and they are very supportable to the Tavern!"

"You really are a clever businessman Don, you haven't stop to amazed me.... if I may say so"

"Thank you Louise but I see no cleverness in that, if anything the clever one is Lisa, and naturally Charlie who he's simply an excellent musician plus the rest who's done a very good job too!"

"Well, it does take some doing Don. Most of all is the marketing, I'd think that's very important!"

"Yes...The rest of the thinking was done the Singalong record company including marketing, without that you wouldn't be able to sell any records at all, and of course some broadcasting from Mercury Radio which would push up the sales for certain!"

"I shall make sure to listen to the radio from tomorrow!"

"I shall do the same Louise, perhaps with a few tears, as I did today when I first I saw the records!"

"Good Lord, I think I am excited as you two. Can you imagine Don, your Tavern will be known all over England, perhaps in time all over the world.......The world's famous Tavern!"

"I thought about that Bob, yes, the music market is vast, all over the world I'd say!"

"Let's toast to their future success then...cheers....cheers, including to your birthday Don!"

"Thank you both you two, you're just like a ray of sunshine to me."

(A lady and a gentleman are just entering the Tavern and walk towards the bar counter)
"Good evening sir, do you think I could speak to Bertie Smith please?"
"Certainly madam, is over there, is the chap with the red bow tie!"
"Thank you very much!"
(They walk towards the table where Bertie and Joe are sitting)
"Good evening Bertie...."
"Good evening madam,,,, what can I do for you?"
"I am Elizabeth Campbell, perhaps you'd be kind enough to take me to Don, I simply would like to say hello!"
"What a surprise.... (**Bertie's getting up)** by all means Elizabeth, please follow me, is over there sitting with two guests... you can see his back!"
"Never mind I'll come another time, I can see is busy at the moment!"
"No.... please follow me, I think he'll be pleased to see you!"
"Did you tell him about our telephone conversation?
"No, actually I thought not to do that, as it would be a nice surprise!"
"Are you sure I won't disturb him?"
"I am positive Elizabeth, please follow me!"
(Bertie taps Don on the shoulder)
"Don sorry to interrupt, but there's a young lady who wishes to say hello to you!"
(Don turns around)
"Goodness me... Elizabeth... What a surprise...Why, why oh why... didn't you tell me that you were coming **(They embrace with a gentle kiss on the cheeks)**
"We were just passing by, and thought to pop in and say hello, I hope I'm not intruding...."
"Thank you Bertie....Oh, can you tell John to bring two clean glasses please? No...no... you are not intruding at all, so nice to see you, please meet my two good friends, Louise and Bob!"
"Nice to meet you both...**(shaking their hands)** and this is my working colleague Brian!"
"This is my ex secretary I would say the greatest beyond any of my expectations, without Elizabeth I could have never have been so successful!
"You are too kind Don.. It's not true, do not believe him!"
"Tell me Brian; are you working in my office?
"Not yet Don... I hope one day soon!"

"Never give up Brian there's a chance for everyone in life! Would you like to have a drink with us, do you mind Louise..Bob?"
"No we don't mind at all, the more the merrier!"
"Thank you Don, but we won't stop for long, just one drink!"
"Nonsense, please take a seat, and tell me some news!"
"There's not much I can say Don, we know you are now on the board of Directors, so you probably know more than me!"
"Perhaps darling, but that it doesn't matter, what matters is that you can to see me and it's nice to see you too. So good health to all of us and prosperity... cheers... you are all wonderful people, and thank you Elizabeth for your good work, I will never forget that.... Cheers!"

Chapter 25

(Meanwhile the situation was not improving for Bertie and Joe)
"Who's Elizabeth then? You seemed to manage to meet some beautiful ladies, you rascal you!"
"No... that was Don's personal secretary when he was working in Dagenham, I must say she's very attractive, he's the rascal one not me! Apparently, she was madly in love with him but he wasn't interested!"
"Bloody hell.. he's fussy, even me I noticed that she's a beauty, you something I think I'm getting like you Bertie, I must stop to look at nice girls, I thought the same when that Miss Ryan gave me the veg order this morning.... yes I thought she a very a good looking lady!"
"You see my friend, you stay by me and you'll start to sample the good taste of the female maturity!"
"Please Bertie, let us look after our own grass, sometimes on the other side it can be a bit dry!"
"Goodness me you sound like a philosopher!"

(Back at Don's table)
"Don I think we better make a move, as we have quite a journey!"
"Did you come by car Brian?
"Yes, I just parked it on the other side of the street, it's an old banger from my dear old father, anyway!"
"Next time park it just outside the Tavern it'll be safer, it was so nice to see you Elizabeth, and please don't make it so long next, and nice to meet you Brian!"
(Another warm embrace) "So nice to see you Don, we all miss you so much, but no doubt I'll see you at the next AGM which it's not far, bye!"
"And a bye, bye from me Don, it was nice to meet you too!"
"Take care you two...bye, bye!"

"So that is your devoted secretary, what a good looking lady, I am surprised that after all these years...you"
"You mean married her? No Louise, Elizabeth is a wonderful person with many qualities, but unfortunately she wasn't my type, although I knew she was fond of me.... but......What more can I say?"

"You are so right Don, it is difficult to find the right partner, that's the problem with marriages, sometimes we think we have the right one and suddenly later we realize that we have the wrong one!"
"Thank you Bob, I really appreciate your interesting opinion!"
"I couldn't agree more with you two, you are so right!"
"Thank you Louise..."
"And thank you for me too... your devoted chauffeur!"
"This calls for another cheers....."

(Bertie and Joe haven't lost their hopes for a reconciliation)
"Rosie I have a complain to make; why do you interfere in other people's business?"
"What's he talking about now? I've got a complaint about you clever clog, for a start look at you, one evening off and you cannot control a couple of drinks, thank God you are not like that when you are on duty...."
"That's alright my darling, when I work I have to see that my customers are standing up properly!"
"Yes, yes... I only wish you would get another job... nine to five that would make a nice change!"
"This job suits me fine and Don is very good to me, furthermore it gives a chance to meet new people every evening... Males and females.... and what's more....."
"Please don't tell us, we all know that he spoils you rotten, and for meeting lots of new people I'd say; you don't have to tell me males and females, we all know that !"
"That might be so, but the real reason is that I'm good at my job, never mind the opposite sex, if I'm looking at them, I consider that some kind of a bonus, or a reward, if you prefer..."
"What reward Bertie? Please tell me another!"
"I will never win with you Rosie!"
"Bertie leave off the arguments for now, (**and whispering)** we said that before... didn't we?
"I'm glad that someone's coming to his senses,. the nap seem to have done some good to you Joe."
"I wasn't really asleep, I was just listening to your good suggestions Rosie, sometimes I think we have to learn how to behave in life from you girls!"
"It seems to me that you and I understand each other much better than someone else!"

"I see!! I think that someone could be me, I didn't know you were so friendly you two! I'll have to keep my eyes open with you my darling"
"Rosie and I have been friends for a long time Bertie, I wouldn't have anyone else looking after my stall while I take a break for my bacon sandwich and a cuppa! Furthermore, don't worry my friend it's not my style stealing wives, especially from friends!"
"You just listen to your friend Bertie,I think he's got more sense than you!
"Stealing wives from friends, are you trying to insinuate that I still wives? That's unfair from both of you, I have to make a cup of tea for myself every morning, while you help out someone else!"
"True, you shouldn't sleep till gone past midday every day then!"
"Be reasonable Rosie, he's a very hard working young lad, look at him poor fellow, he 's even hurt his eye doing his duty! By the way, it's very quite around here, perhaps it's about time I show my hidden talent too.... **(and turning to Charlie)** Charlie, do you remember the last song we wrote together?"
"You mean...`I'm lost without you`
That's alright Charlie, can you dig out the score, I don't remember the words very well....!"
"There you are Joe, I think you will it on page seventy six...."
(So Charlie begins with the intro.........)

(Joe grabs the mike and sings his old soapy lovey-dovey song pretending as if nothing has happened)

"It all begun with that first smile/I was so shy just for a while/You look so beautiful so fine/I knew at once that you were mine!/It all begun with our first kiss/I thought that was some kind of bliss/You never made me feel that blue/But now I'm lost without you!`
`You were my only one possession/within my heart a true obsession/I loved you through and through/My life is empty without you!`
`I often play that magic song/Called; Love Little Love Me Long/But what's the use, now I feel blue/
Because I'm lost without you!/Because I'm lost without you/Because I'm lost without you!"
(Although Joe had not sung in public since school days, that's where he met Lisa, it has been known they were the perfect duo, he seemed to have impressed the punters and the girls for that matter.)

Chapter 26

(Even Louise, Don and Bob were impressed with Joe's performance)

"That's what I like to hear in my Tavern, participating in good music, actually I enjoy seeing people taking part in the show, makes a lot of difference than listening someone arguing!"
"I couldn't agree with you more Don, that's what I call a good friendly atmosphere, I really loved his voice and style!"
"Glad to hear your appreciation Louise, actually that was the very first time I heard Joe singing, I'm very impressed myself too!"
"Maybe he should take Lisa's place and sing a few ballads that would give a break to the dancers making the show more interesting Don."
"It's not a bad idea Louise, but I don't know whether Joe would do that, knowing his Lisa would be singing somewhere else!"
"I don't think that would work, may I make a suggestion, yes a simple suggestion from an old chauffeur; Forget those ideas, the Piccadilly Tavern was made to be with the dancers and the occasional singer for a sing along, that is the great atmosphere of this place..... agree?
"Yes I agree Bob, and thank you for your suggestion!"
"In this case I am incline to agree with you two gentlemen!"
"And so let us have another glass of bubbly.... Cheers Louise...cheers Bob..."

(Meanwhile Bertie is complimenting Joe for his superb performance)
"That was really good Joe, your interpretation almost got me back to normal **(and whispering)** but.. but you didn't get many applause like your sweetheart gets... pardon me... ex sweetheart. Mind you the song was a bit of creeping, I don't mean to lower your esteem, or shall I say pride? but if you ask me, perhaps it would have been better if you had said `sorry darling`...please take me back! Don't take my opinion too personal. It's only a suggestion!"
(Smiling and ignoring Bertie's remarks but winking and nodding)
"Actually I wrote that song, quite a few years ago, it was during the time we used to go to that night club Bertie, you must remember that.. we used to have a hell of a good time, you remember that blond usherette that sold cigarettes and cigars, I thought I had a crush on her, but as usual she did fancy you!"

"Oh yes...yes...No... No... she did fancy you Joe you really had a crush on her, I thought she fancied me first, but I was wrong!"
"Thank God for that, it makes a change for you to say that I am right!"
"Look Joe...(**whispering)** first you tell me, no more lies, no more comments, no more arguments, and now you come up with a story that doesn't make any sense at all, she never going to believe you mate, if she heard it!"
"Well Bertie **(whispering**) I really don't know what to do or say anymore, I've used up all my good efforts, are we insane?!"
"No Joe, they we're not insane.... try and relax for a few minutes and see what we can come up with..... the world's still intact so we haven't lost the battle yet!"
"Too right... I think we lost the war!"
"Lucy I can't hear what they are saying as they are whispering most of the time, really I shouldn't take any notice as I'm sure they are talking rubbish... I heard night club... Joe's never been to a night club in his life, he doesn't know the meaning of the word!"
"Yes Lisa... I heard usherette selling cigarettes.... crush on a blonde, what a lot of rubbish, I just can't make it out.....
"I heard that too Lucy, I am so pleased that you couldn't hear our conversation, maybe you are going deaf!"
"No we are not deaf Bertie, and haven't lost our memory, we can hear well, and we remember well!
"Sorry Lucy... I didn't mean it the way you think, what I meant was perhaps there's too much noise in here tonight, and you couldn't catch what we were saying......and......
"I know...I know... Bertie I do understand, but let me remind you, we can hear, we remember well and we won't forget too easily... right Lisa?
"You know something girls, I really feel confused, I just don't know what you lot are talking about!"
"Oh nothing in particular Rosie, just a simple game we were playing last night with Nosey Pete, which in the end we had to agree, that it was only joking.....
"I suppose you will try to explain it to in a better way, because I am still confused LIsa."
"It's true Rosie... it's not really all that important.....
"If you say that Lisa, I believe you!"
"I feel sorry for you Joe, I'm still convinced that beautiful song of yours would have done the job, but it failed, and so the night club adventure,

but never lose faith and hope, our victory will soon be here, don't forget, we haven't lost the war and neither the battle yet."

"I hope you are right Bertie, I'm getting a bit depressed with the whole situation, what with Lisa taking up this job, I'll have to cut out my pleasures, like coming in here, I just could not come in here knowing that she wouldn't be around, I just couldn't face it!"

"Don't worry my friend, in any case there's plenty more fish in the sea, we can always go fishing together if you wish...."

"I don't really like your sense of humour Bertie, instead of making me laugh, it makes me cry!"

"Don't take it like that.... Take my brother for instance... just look at him over there, laughing and joking with his friends, you know he really fancies Lucy... did you know that?"

"No I didn't know that... how did you find out?"

"I reckon one of these days he's going to pop the question, I know for the fact that he keeps her photograph on the back door of his wardrobe, crafty old bagger, he thinks I don't know..."

"I can't believe it Bertie... after all the things he says about her, and the nasty way she treats him sometimes, I am surprise he won't give up his chances, well, they might love each other just like a platonic love... Hey look who's coming in... it's Merlin the busker..."

"Yes Joe... he told me this morning that he probably would come and see us after his gig!"

"Hello Merlin.. what brings you here tonight?"

Hello Joe... I promised Bertie that I would pop in after the gig in Leicester Square!"

"I see you have a friend with you, and I see he's a musician too for what he's carrying!"

"Yes Joe, this is my friend Mario from Italy, we met in Rome a few years ago during a music festival, and since then we kept in contact!"

"Hello you all... my name is Mario... you have many, many friends, eh.. Merlin?"

"Yes Mario.. and they all very kind to me, this is Bertie, who I used to gig many moons ago, he used to play drums...."

"Nice to meet you Mario... they were not a proper drums but they sounded like it...."

"This night club... is nice Merlin..."

"Mario this is not a night club, it's a Tavern... or shall I say a typical old style show house, where people of all class can enjoy at a modest price a good pint of Ale, laughing and singing with the girls at the sound of the old Joanna, it's the honky tonky piano"

"Yes, I know in Italian we call it Piano Verticale.......Oh look Merlin... they make record too, that is fantastic.... bello...bello... "

"Oh yes.. congratulations girls... Lisa of course... Lisa is Joe fiance Mario..."

"Oooohh... bella... bella fidanzata , and all the others all belle, very beautiful"

"Okay Mario calm down, calm down.. you are in England now...if you're unlucky enough you will find one for yourself!"

"You say lucky not unlucky Bertie... me will find one!"

"Yes of course Mario... you will find many......By the sound he like girls a lot....Me too."

"Yes Mario like girls.... God made girls for boys, like me make music for lovers!"

"That is nice Mario, very romantic......we call girls trouble makers...Only joking Mario!"

"Mario don't listen to Bertie, he's very upset about his black eye!"

"Oh yes.. I thought it was very unusual to see you with dark glasses this morning Bertie..."

"And I told you it was because of the sun... it's true Merlin! This happened this afternoon!"

"Me see... your friends all very gentlemen.... very nice all!"

"Thank you Mario, at last someone tells the truth about us..."

"Hello Merlin... so nice to see you here..."

"Hello Peter..... let me introduce my Italian friend Mario....Mario this is my very good friend Peter, he always looks after me when I play in the Market!"

"Please meeting you Peter...."

"So you have been around the Country Merlin, in the past few months, how's life treating you then, do you still live in Brighton, and any addition to the family yet?"

"No.. we can't afford it, Carolyn has a job, and we just bought a small place, we have a little mortgage you know what is like to pay back the borrowed money, but we can't complain!"

"That's nice to hear that you have both settled down...."

"Yes we are quieter now... during the summer we are mostly based in Brighton as we do some gigs on the beach, she's a good singer too... you know?"

"I am so pleased for you Merlin..... Hey.... you remember that song we wrote together and we played it so many times... called `From my heart I love you so!`"
"Of course I do, we played it tonight in Leicester Square, actually we had to do it twice because people liked it so much... Mario made a very good job of the middle instrumental part with his sax... what about it Bertie?
"Well... I would like to performed in here tonight and (**whispering)** I'm going to do it for my beautiful Rosie, and I would like Mario to do a special instrumental improvisation bit, because I like the sax very much, no need to try it, Charlie knows it because we done it a couple of times in the past!"
"Yes that song was molto much great, my compliments to you Bertie, good write song, people like that song very very lot, people ask for more... we say BIS.."
"What's a bis then Merlin?
"Yes Pete... bis means an anchor... in other words do it again!"
"Mario.. you make sure you play with a lot Sentimento... feeling..."
"Me know Bertie, me will do that..... plenty sentimento......Sorry Bertie me no speak good English"
"Don't worry Mario, Merlin don't speak very good English too....
"Many thanks....my good friend... just make sure you remember the words, and keep the timing right, don't look at the girls when you are singing otherwise you lose the concentration....
"I like that Merlin I shall do my very best, you know I can do it!"
"I heard you are going to sing Bertie, I hope you are not going to make a spectacle of yourself!"
"Well.... as you heard I might as well, make an introduction: Ladies and gentlemen, I will now sing a special song for my adorable wife which I wrote many moons ago.... Go on Merlin let's have it, and Mario... show these people what you can do with your sax... keep it softly and adagio to start.. Charlie and Merlin will follow with his guitar.... off we go.....

Chapter 27

(Bertie sings)

"If I could catch a rainbow/I do it just for you/and share with you its beauty/on the days you're feeling blue!/If I could build a mountain/I'd call it by your name/I think you ought to know though/From my heart I love you so!

If I could have your troubles/I would toss them into the sea/But all these things I'm finding/ Too impossible for me!

I cannot build a mountain/Or catch a rainbows end/But I still want you to know though/From my heart I love you so!"

(Mario comes in with a solo sax and although the song is only halfway, everyone applaud and whistles. Bertie and Merlin look at each other with a smile, confirming that they have something precious in their hands, ending with more applause, while Rosie approaches Bertie......)

"Well done you rascal you, I'm very impressed and proud, I suppose we can call a truce, or water under a bridge, all is forgiven darling, you are still my macho man...!"

"Do you mean only for a few days or forever?"

"You know I mean forever.... Provided you are more careful down in the cellar... you silly boy, at least it happened when you were drunk!"

"Thank you sweetheart that was really dedicated to you. Darling I never drink in this place? I will really be more careful next time!"

"I know my love... this was one of your rare dedications... we should make it a special day! Except I still think about the accident in the cellar, well...... I am not convinced yet, I'd say; one hundred per cent."

"Rosie darling, I wouldn't force you to believe about that unfortunate accident, but the cellar was built in the seventeen century and believe me it has now become a very dangerous place to keep wine and beer, I did have a word with Don to make it more safer, he promised he would!"

"Well.... that make sense Bertie..."

"What else can I say? Only that I love you Rosie..!"

"And I love you too darling..!"

"I just cannot believe Lisa (**whispering**) how he can get away so easy!"

"Yes.. you are right Lucy... I think Rosie loves him far too much, what else could it be?"

"You have a point there Lisa, he certainly has that particular charm... coming back slowly"
"Please Lucy, don't make me cry! I do still love him I suppose I always will, the stubborn sod! "
"Sorry Lisa... I didn't mean it and I am so happy that you still love him!"
"Oh I know Lucy... and I am so happy for Rosie too!"
"Don't worry Lisa, I'm sure your happy hour will come for you very soon!"

(Meanwhile at the birthday's table)
"Your charming barman has a good voice too, so you have two male singers all of a sudden, don't you think so Don? Actually you should give him a chance to perform on that stage with his friends now and then!"
"Please Louise, Bertie is very good behind the bar and looking after the staff. Now he even does my book keeping, I spent hours teaching him and he's good at it, so he has taken a weight off my back, he's a clever boy, at this rate he will be running the tavern for me, and to be honest, without him around here I'd be lost... anyway I don't really want him in two places, further more being too near the dancers he might lose his concentration, I know what he's like with beautiful girls!"
"I understand Don, you mean that would create marital problems?"
"Well Louise, if you want to put it like that, I'm incline to agree with you!"

(Bob has a crackling smile and likes to give his opinion too)

"He reminds me of my younger days..."
"Were you a womaniser too Bob... and created marital problems... so to speak?"
"I might have been, I don't think you know me at all Louise, mind you I did calm down when I was over twenty five, you do change when you start having responsibilities, anyway I am pleased with myself, more than anything, I've got a good job, and that it's very important for my life!"
"Yes I know you have a good job and as for knowing you; Well... I can only say that you are a true gentleman Bob, how long we've known each other... twelve years I think!"
"Yes we are nearly there, don't forget that we had a present from the Simpsons on our tenth anniversary!"
"A present? The Simpson family must be really generous, please don't tell us what it was, otherwise I'm going to be jealous!"

"We might as well tell you Don, no bones about it... eh Bob?"
"Go on Louise speak up..."
"Okay, they gave us a little cottage each in their grounds for our own use, with all expenses paid for as long as we are employed with them, not very far from the Manor, Don can we have another bottle of Bubbly please?"
"No problems dear... I'll go an order it... won't be long...(**mumbling along)** A cottage each eh? In the manor grounds... lucky people, I am sure they have deserved it, at first I thought they live together, but it looks like they live in separate places... Still, I'm so happy for them!"
"Hi Don... I see you are mumbling to yourself, are you alright?
"Yes John I am alright, I was just thinking about something, be a good chap, get me a bottle of bubbly in the ice bucket please, make sure a vintage one, and put it in my little book of expenses, I will take it to the table myself!"
"Will you need clean glasses Don?"
"No don't bother, we shall use the same.... on second thoughts, yes please give me some clean glasses, sorry to mess you about John!"
"Oh, that's okay.... Don!"

(**Meanwhile Rosie approaches Lisa)**
"Lisa my darling, I think I'll have to disappoint you regarding that offer you made me, I seriously thought about it very carefully, I think I was a bit too hasty, when I said I would accept, perhaps I've got too much to lose, therefore I'll stay with my trouble maker, he'll be more safe under my control, you know what I mean!"
"I do understand Rosie, this is why I told you to think about it as your situation it's not like mine, you are married to him and that says a lot, don't forget I am still single.....But for you.....it would have been a big step to do, never mind, we won't lose our friendship, I can assure you!"
"You bet your boots we won't, that would upset me tremendously!"

(**Bertie's approaching Rosie)** "Thank you darling I knew you couldn't stay away from me and I know for the fact that you feel seasick when travelling on boats!"
"True, so you better behave yourself from now on and stop rocking the boat yourself!"
"That's it Rosie put your foot down and show him who's the boss!"
"You better stick to your business my dear bruv..."

(Lucy comes along)

"Oh Rosie... I am so happy for you, I hope he will take you somewhere nice for dinner, I know the place, where you will both have a great time and that is at the Mayfair Hotel, where you can have a candlelight dinner with the music of Harry Boy.... is very famous you know?

"That sounds exciting Lucy... I think I'd like that..... What do you think Bertie?

"Hemm.. Yes that sounds perfect... Rosie, what a good idea Lucy, I never knew you were fond of Harry Boy's music, as a matter of fact he sings and plays the clarinet, I've never heard him playing but someone told me that he's very, very good!"

"Yes he is, and now, that she has one of our records, you'll have to buy her a gramophone, I've got one.... they so pleasant to listen to, anyway I will lend you the latest of Harry Boy's record if you like.... plus I've got a few more from my father collection, you can borrow some, if you like!"

"What a lot of good suggestions Lucy, I really do appreciate them, yes Rosie tomorrow we might go and see if we can buy one... gramophone that is! You know something Lucy? As much as I like music I never thought of buying one before, you really convinced me.....Oh..I really would like to listen to that Harry Boy again, I'll keep that in mind...thank you Lucy!"

"Hold on my love, I thought you never listened to him before?"

"Oh.... I forgot to tell you Rosie, I think I heard him on the radio!"

"Oh... I see.... I wonder what he's like......."

Chapter 28

(Lucy's back on the stage with Lisa)

"I heard that Lucy, we finally got our revenge poor old Bertie, I bet he didn't like those suggestions, they are going to cost him a fortune, dinner at the Mayfair and a new gramophone....ha,ha,ha, serves him right!"
"Too right, he's lucky really. He got away lightly and we got away without murdering him...He can carry on living now....ha,ha,ha,"
"We might as well close the subject now Lucy.... it's all history!"
"Yes, still... I am very happy for them.... I only wish that something would happen to me too, that would be a big change in my life.... **(Pete just stands behind Lucy)**
"I haven't heard anything, but I had that sort of feeling myself Lucy!"
"I don't understand Pete, what sort of feeling?"
"For a start I'm going to change my attitude toward people, I feel it's about time a dish out some apologies, for all the problems I've caused, I find it a bit boring now, as no one gets upset anymore, I see they are only laughing, when I say my daily critics!"

(Bertie's covering his black eye with his hand and looks at two special girls)
"I think I'd like to join you with some special apologies dear bruv!"
"Hush...Hush... dear bruv, **(And whispering) It's** about Rosie and you know who, I can tell you that you don't have to worry about.... because nothing happened, will tell you later... the true story...."
"Thanks bruv...I appreciate that.....you are a genius!"
"As I was saying Lucy, the girls... and you lot **(looking at the crowd)** I would like to apologise for any hurt I've cause to any of you....."
"Apologies accepted my friend....."
"Thank you Greasy, but please let me finish **(and turning toward the bar counter, he grabs the flowers vase and kneels in front of Lucy)**
"I am truly sorry Lucy for every malicious feeling I've caused you, I'm only borrowing these flowers, hoping you'll understand my loving feelings for you, I have loved you since the first day I met you... will you accept these flowers with my sincere words....? In simple terms; I love you Lucy!!

(Complete silence for a minute as friends and crowd are simply flabbergasted, a proposition of love without knowing the answer, a refusal would have made Pete a laughing stock of the year, but Lucy totally blushing with a few tears, and looking definitively bewildered ....replies with a smile..........)

"I am speechless Peter, yes of course I accept them including every word you said, I am a bit confused, and please don't make me blush more than I am in front of these lovely people, what else can I say? The feeling is mutual or I better say.... I love you too!"

(Clapping and whistling from all the crowd for the wonderful event)

"Lucy I can only promise that my troubles are now nonexistent any longer, I feel I am a new man from the moment I heard you saying `I love you,` I waited so long I'm sure you're going to make me the happiest husband in town....Good Lord I hope I am not dreaming!"

"Hi Lucy.. I can confirm that, my rascal bruv.. keeps your photograph on the back of his wardrobe!"

"Thank you brother, that was a lovely secret that I thought no one knew, but I'm glad that it came out in the open and yes, I do treasure that photo, I think I shall have in a frame now...!"

"I would rather see one in a frame of us two Peter!"

"Of course my darling Lucy, I'm sure that won't be long and it will be one in a white dress!"

Oh, darling... I just can't wait for the big day... my mum will be over the moon too, knowing that at last I will be settling down!"

"I'm sure we'll be so happy together because I love you so much! **(and turning to the crowd)** Help yourself with a drink my friends, and please no doubles....ha,ha,ha,ha!"

"Little rascal... he's starting already cutting corners....."

"Marriage is very expensive Stanley.... you should know you've been married three times!"

"Please don't remind me, you'll only spoil my evening.... Cheers young lovers.... all the best!"

(It didn't take long for Charlie to rustle a well known old song for them to sing as a duet, so away he goes with the old Joanna giving them the first notes of: `We are so happy and in love` exchanging faithfulness and true love. Everyone cheers the new happy couple including Louise, Bob and Don)

"There you go Louise another happy couple, I must say that in the very short time of the Tavern, I've seen quite a few loves old and new being reborn, some lasting and some vanishing like a dream, I only wish my first and true love would have lived longer, but sadly for some peculiar reasons, it vanished like a cloud after a thunderstorm....sigh... However, that isn't the end of the world as you can see, these are simply facts of life.... which no doubt sometimes they can be very hurtful!"

"Where did you meet your first love Don and how old were you?"

"I rather not talk about it, because when I do, it upsets me for a couple of days, and that's makes me feel miserable, perhaps....perhaps....I still love her, yes I do love her so much, but I suppose the past cannot be brought back!"

"Go on Don have another glass of bubbly, and give us a smile, as you said it's not the end of the world... just think a lot of people out there are worse off than you and I!"

"You are right Bob, and I would like to add again that it was really a pleasure to meet you and Louise... well.... you made me feel really.. happy, although I envy you a little bit... maybe that's the wrong word, I should't have said it, up to yesterday my life was work, work, work, and I think that's not right, I've come to the conclusion that there are other things in life other than being committed night and day to the flipping work, naturally when I saw you and Louise taking some time off, and enjoying yourself even for a simple theatrical pleasure, I'm sure it refreshes your mind, that's why I've used the word... envy!"

"It is true Don, we do try to forget about our duties now and then, it does gives us more power to work the next day!"

"Thank you, I must say I feel almost like a new man, I'm sure it's not the bubbly talking! You have given me a new lease of life"

"No... it's you talking Don... I do understand how you feel......And tell me Don... what about Elizabeth you secretary!"

"Yes, as I said before, she was crazy about me Louise, she was so kind, very committed to her job and very loyal, but there's something that she's just not my type, she was very upset when I left, she didn't even turned up for the opening, so here I am still a free bachelor!"

"And what about the widow who looks after your property in Dagenham?"

"Who...Jackie?....She's lovely too, but I wouldn't think she's after a new husband! She gave me the impression that she's very happy on her own, some women are quite content when they become widows, maybe because they can survive on their own better than men."

"What's the reasons then Don?"

"Simple really, most women can cook, can saw, can do the house work, the gardening, and many other chores... better than a man in all aspects.... and they can survive without sex, please correct me if I'm wrong Bob!"

"I suppose you have a good point there Don and I admire you... for being so honest, I'll tell you something, you'll never be on your own, your friendliness will be rewarded one day and your dream will come true!"

"My goodness you sound like a fortune teller Bob, just the same, I thank you for the encouragement and I hope you are going to be right... I have been rewarded so far with my jobs and now this beautiful place surrounded by good people, and as we are on the subject, e few days ago they completed my living headquarters on the second and third floor, I have now a four bedroom apartment all to myself, with all the amenities I need, overlooking regent street, I hope it's not going to be too big for me, mind you it'll be easier to accommodated my lot from Ireland when they visit me!"

"What about your first floor Don, have you got plans for that?"

"Oh yes Bob, I'm thinking to turn that into a conference room with private Bar and other facilities."

"You certainly never stop thinking up new ideas..Eh.... Don?"

"Well, I'll be honest with you Bob, some nights I find it very difficult to fall asleep, naturally if I had a wife to nag me, I wouldn't have time to think up these ideas!"

"You just reminded me when first I met you Don, full of inventiveness!"

"Thank you Louise, and I still see in you, that clever look in you because you take notice of everything I say, that's how you were.. yes you were always interested in anything I would say!"

"True Don... because you never used to talk rubbish.......Your conversations were magnificent! "

"Thank you Louise I do appreciate your good memory...."

"Then Don may I propose a toast, not only to your birthdays but also to your new accommodation?"

"Cheers Bob...Cheers Louise.. to your good health!"

Chapter 29

(Meanwhile Bertie, Rosie, Lisa, Joe, Merlin, and Mario are sitting drinking Peter's generous round of drinks and talking about the two lovers. Lucy and Pete seem to have become the talk of the Tavern. Who'd have thought something like that to happened so quickly? Of course that brought some interesting comments.)

"Love can play some strange tricks sometimes...Don't you think so Joe?"
"Yes Bertie you can say that again..."
"I'm not so sure Bertie, sometimes tricks like that can bring some troubles!"
"I don't think you are right Joe... it might be in a few years time, after the eternal ring!"
"You can' t really forecast anything like that, it can happen anytime Merlin!
"Yes Merlin that's the best answer....You can't forecast the future really"
"I say no many troubles but plenty love... that make all problems go away.... Say Italians via...via, and plenty amore, night and day!"
"Well said Mario.....That's not bad at all.... is that the Italian attitude?
"Me understand.... attitudine.. yes Italian family very attached to family love... not always in bed!"
"You mean Italian families are very family orientated...Both ways?"
"Yes... many always together... for many years...And have dinners all together every day!"
"Oh... I got you Mario, I think I go and live in Italy.....I like hot dinners, maybe the answer is the Vino, eh?""
"Yes the Vino molto importante in Italy... But No good to live there now Joe... Mussolini is very tiranno.. dittatore.....how do you say.."
"Oh yes..we know Mussolini is a tyrant... is a dictator....
"Yes... dictator.... what he say..we must do. no complaining. Black shirts carry big stick and guns!"
"Well... we better stay here then , only the police carry the stick and don't beat people up!
"Yes much better.... people here very kind.....and life more easy!"

"Alright enough of politics... now then, we know that love is crazy, why don't we do a crazy song, say how about that song called `Crazy for you`?"
"Yes me know song from film Fred Upstairs......in Roma cinema"
"That's alright I sung that in school with a beautiful young girl.. we done a duet, I wonder who that girl was then?"
"Yes... You know that girl was me, we sung it as a duet together... are you satisfy now Joe?"
"Come on you two, forget your problems for a few minutes, and behave yourself, this is show business! People is waiting for more entertainment! Sorry Rosie I had to say something......!"
"You said the right thing Bertie!"

(And so Merlin decides to do another performance)

"Right let's get going, Charlie you know that song `Crazy for you`?"
"Yes I do Merlin....."
"Okay then..... Joe and Lisa you just do it as you did it in school, Mario will coming now and then with his sax, and the middle instrumental will be sung by the girls as a Charleston tempo. Okay let's get started, as a swing, and ending as a swing too.... Okay you lot.... one, two, three, and four.....
(Joe sings)
"Crazy for you, crazy for you I'm so crazy for you/What can I do, when you're not here, I feel ever so blue**!/(Lisa sings)** Crazy for you, don't ask me why, we're so happy you and I/Crazy for you it's really true,/I'm so crazy for you!
(Joe sings) Your eyes can quite hypnotize me/Your smile can truly revive me/By any doubt of what might be/I'm not too blind to see!/
(Lisa sings) Crazy for you, tell me you care, don't let me in despair/What will I do, without your love, I'm so crazy for you!
(The girls sings and dance) Crazy for you, crazy for you, we're so crazy for you/What can we do, when you're not there, we feel ever so blue!
(Lisa sing) Your words can easily seduce me/You know which way where to find me/You know my problems, yes you do/Can't you see I love you!
(Joe sings) Crazy for you, what will I do, if you love me no more?/Sure I will be, lonely and sad, Once again like before!
(Lisa & Joe sing as duet) This is your chance don't let it go, let it be pure romance!/Give me your hand/Please hold me tight/Let our love have no end/I'm so crazy for you/ it's true, I'm so crazy for you! For you!

(With that song they seem to have forgotten, what caused their silly rift, admitting that their love should have no end, because they are crazy for each other, people really appreciated that performance, the crowd never seem to stop applauding. Thanks to Merlin for a such bright idea.)

"I never thought I needed your help Merlin to get us to sing together, many thanks, I was a bit out of order with her!"

"So I gathered Joe... I knew I could do something to break the ice, to be honest I seem to have the knack to unite young lovers after their war of words, whether with my musical touch or my ideas!"

"Thank you Merlin, you are a wonderful musician, we shall look forward to your next visit, you must come and see us... again.. but now I have a lot to discuss with this young man..."'

"I am so glad for you both Lisa, you are such a lovely couple!"

"I wish you did that to me and Lucy long time ago my good friend!"

"You never mentioned Lucy to me Peter, otherwise I could have done something, you are a lovely couple too!"

"I tried a couple of times but I didn't know where to start.....

"Never mind my good friend, I wish you a lot of happiness, and don't forget to send me an invitation for the big day, I'm sure Carolyn would look forward to come too!

"And me.. will come from Italy too!"

"Of course Merlin you can count on that..... and you Mario too!"

"Me wait very much invitation.... grazie and thank you.

(All this was being watch by the birthday table and they seemed to have enjoyed it too.)

"I did enjoy that Don, without a doubt that was our second show tonight, which I can honestly say it was the best of the two, don't you think so Bob?"

"I certainly agree with you Louise, that was superb, and look at them how they are chatting away, it seems they are having a party!"

"I really enjoy this atmosphere Bob... no arguments, no jealousy's scenes... yes is what I always wanted.... don't you think it's nice Louise?"

"Yes it is Don, and I am so pleased for you... one thing that still bother me, and I say this with sincerity, it's the departure of Lisa.. I hope she will change her mind now that it seems things are getting better!"

"Yes they seem to have improved they relation, but not one hundred per cent Louise, as she hasn't said anything yet, I am keeping my fingers crossed and I am hoping the same as you, but for the moment I have no other alternative, but to announce her departure...."
"In the meantime can we have another bottle please? These bottles must have a hole on the bottom or is it us drinking too much?
"I must admit I think I am exciding my quantity, but what the heck.... I am enjoying myself and it helps me to forget....."
"And this one will be on us Don... no arguments... okay?
"I was the first to suggest it, and really!! I can't take your money as I still owe your parents one month rental... as when I left, if I had paid the rent I wouldn't have been able, to pay for my transport, however, I did say I would sent it to your father, but I simply forgot....ha,ha,ha,ha...!
"I can see in your smile that you are lying Don, this is not you saying that you do something and then you do not keep your word....."
"You think what you like.... in the meantime I'm going to order another bottle....

(Don goes to the bar to order another bottle of Champagne for his celebration, at the same time he bangs on the counter for a special announcement.)

"Ladies and gentlemen, I can see that we are having quite an exciting evening tonight, and rather full of genius musicality, I must say very enjoyable too, just the kind of evening I wanted for the anniversary of the Piccadilly Tavern, and without you all this place wouldn't be what it is today, plus I have been able to combine this evening with my birthday, rest assure I will not tell you my age...ah,ha,ha,ha.. at this point I would like to take this opportunity to thank you all for making it a really successful place, in saying that, I think there something missing, usually there's always a landlady with the landlord, but sadly you'll have to make do with just an old landlord. Finally, and very sadly I must tell you that our delightful Lisa has given us her notice, she will be leaving the Tavern in four weeks time, this is not because she doesn't like you or me, on the contrary she loves us all...."
"I'll drink to that...."
"If you don't mind Bertie...... Yes... our darling Lisa....she's going to promote and upgrade her superb career as a singer, which she deserves so much. Lisa is not only a good friend, but I feel somehow she's part of

the family, she has given us so much pleasure with her voice and her enchanted songs, giving us the chance to forget our worries and troubles.....**(looking at Lisa)** We will certainly miss you my darling and let us hope to see you back pretty soon, after all, this is where you belong, **(takes his handkerchief and makes out he blows his nose)** I'm sorry I'm getting a bit soft in my old age.... Anyway.....as tonight is more or less my special night, I would like to ask Lisa to sing that beautiful song she sung to me when I interviewed her, which really impressed me so much, and by the way tomorrow, you will find it in the record shops coupled with our famous Charleston; `Love and Champagne` Lisa do you remember it?"

"Yes.. how can I forget that! `If I would give my heart to someone` **(and looking at Joe)** it does bring back sweet memories to me too......Please Charlie........

(Lisa sings)

"If I would give my heart to someone/Nothing would stop me to say/You truly are my special one/You keep me going night and day!/If I give you all my possessions/The only reason I see/That you mine true obsession/Please never leave us, stay by me!

Just you, I want you so, more than you know, you are my man/ Just you, can flick your eye, quick as a fly, you've got your dame!

If I would give my love to someone/That someone would have to be/My only love, my only one/ Exclusively for me!/Please take my heart is yours forever/This is your chance and mine too/We've got the world and we'll never/ Tear it apart I love you..And so in love for us two..Oh, I love you..!"

(During the end Joe couldn't take his eyes of Lisa, must have been the last two paragraphs that touched his heart and made him realize how much he loves her. The applauds are just unbelievable, Lisa never had an ovation as such, Don is the first to congratulate her giving her a gentle peck on her cheek.......)

Chapter 30

"All this wasn't planned my dear Louise, but I am equally very happy how things have folded in a nice way, ill parting with our sweet Lisa would have been disastrous and sad!"

"We are with you dear Don, and so pleased with everything we've seen so far, maybe the time has come to give you the unexpected surprise for your birthday!"

"But Louise.... you already wished me happy birthday more than once tonight, and that was more that anyone could ask, really....!"

"No Don, this is more than any specific presents, it is probably something that you would never have thought in a million years......**(and walking toward Lisa, Louise takes by her hand and;)** Congratulations darling Lisa and that goes the same to your partner too... **(looking at Joe)** who I believe is Joe, I'm quite sure you'll be very happy together, you'll make a very nice couple indeed.....and I think this is a great opportunity for me to tell you what I have in store for you Lisa **(and looking at Don)** Would you be so kind to join us.... you old softy?"

"Are you talking to me Louise?"

"Of course I'm talking to you.. **(Don goes next to Louise who gets hold of his hand too)..** So here I am between two nice people who lived in the unknown, I'm say this because..... Lisa is about time that you ought to know a little secret, that I kept into my heart for quite a long time, I might as well say; years, **(looking and pointing her finger on Don chest)** sweetheart I know it's going to be quite a shock for you too Don, but sooner or later it had to be done, I just can't keep it inside me any longer, **(the crowd stand silently, bewildered and wondering)** Lisa.... Don and I are your real parents, enough of this Liverpool accident, which is not true, I am sorry to be so blunt. Please understand that this is a serious matter, naturally I did ask the permission of your adopted parents to be able to disclose such news to you... who they kindly agreed.......

(The crowd is still very silent and so Louise tells her little story, of course Louise is sheding a few tears, Don is speechless and Lisa is petrify and confused looking at Louise and then..........)

"Yes, when Don arrived from Ireland came to live in my parent's house. Don and I became very good friends, so close was our friendship, that very soon we fell in love. I was only seventeen years old, and when my father found out about our wonderful affair, he told Don to pack his bags and leave the house and never show his face again, I was at the college that day and when I came home I was told that he had to go back to Ireland very quickly at least for a couple of months. Few months later they found out I was pregnant, that was a shock for them, my mother told me how my father dealt with Don, so an unmarried young girl pregnant? Yes, it was a sin, and to save themselves from the old fashioned Irish embarrassment they decided to send me to a trustworthy relative to have my baby, and that was beautiful Lisa, who they gave her away for adoption, they also forbid me to have any contact with Don, should he ever contact me, but we lost touch, it was only by pure chance when the Tavern opened that I saw his name in a newspaper, that's how I found him.....

"Quite an unbelievable story darling...... so far.... so true....

"Yes Don, it is indeed so true **(and looking at Lisa)** And when you came to this world darling there was nothing I could do to make things different. As time went by, I managed to meet your adopted parents many times, but you never saw me, I did watch you growing up gracefully and kept my eyes on you regularly. I was tremendously proud of you for all your achievements you gained during your school days and I am so proud of your adopted parents **(more tears)** they knew exactly how to treat a child, although they never had any children themselves!"

(Lisa embrace Louise and Don with tears all over their faces. Don trembling and excited confirms;)

"Yes Lisa, I can vouch every word Louise said. Unfortunately one day I was helping Louise, to do her home work, and to thank me she gave me a little kiss, that's how it all started, and that was the kiss of love, we loved each other so much, that we lost our heads. One day the father saw us kissing, unbeknown to us. The next day he took me on the side and told me that his little princess was only seventeen, still at school and far too young to have a relationship, he told me to pack my bags and find myself some other mugs. I felt completely distraught but never lost faith, some friends took me in for a few nights, but I promised I should not hurt Louise parents feelings, as she was too young and too precious to them, although she had stolen my heart forever, the truth was that I never knew that I left her pregnant, even if I had known, I couldn't have done much, as I was penniless!"

"My grandfather did that to you Don? He must have been very strict!"

"Yes he was very strict sweetheart because he loved his little princess... your mama too much, but in spite of all that, they were very generous to me, they treated me like one of the family, that's the truth. I suppose your mum and I are to blame for it, we were in love, sometime mistakes can happen... you know?"

"Yes I do agree with you father...."

"Please don't make me cry...

"Why not? Sooner or later I'll have to get use to this, father!"

"Lisa darling we won't stop you to love your adopted parents, I know you love them as much as they love you!"

"Yes I know mum and I am so happy, I must go to Joe now, as I have something to tell him!"

"Joe... I'm sure you'll be happy to know that I won't take that new job, I feel I have more responsibility now with four parents to look after!"

"Yes I do agree darling, but may I remind you that you've got an extra person to look after and that is a future husband... if you don't mind!"

"Oh Joe... do you really mean that?

"Of course I do darling, but first I shall have to ask permission of your parents!"

"As long as you don't do it like Bertie, he asked my Nan instead of my father!"

"Oh Rosie! Did he really?"

Yes Lisa, he was afraid of a refusal, between us, he was scared stiff of my father, I think it was his moustaches, in fact Bertie used to address him as the general...

That's very funny Rosie. Did you hear that Joe?

(Don and the rest were listening too, every word being said and Louise and Don still wiping his nose and tears)

"Did you hear that Don?"

"Yes Louise, I am so happy (**and whispering)** will it last?"

"Of course it will Don, they have been in love since she was seventeen...ha,ha,ha,ha...."

"Oh... I've got you now, you mean our love lasted that long?"

"Yes darling since I was seventeen, and you can see I am still here with you!"

"You mean that you and Bob.... or Bob and you...."

"Go on Bob.. put him out of his misery..."

"No problems Louise. Don let me tell you something; First let me introduce myself properly; I am Lord Simpson, but I'll always be Bob to you. I must confess that I've known the story for a long time, and, I promised Louise that I would have helped her to sort it out, so I did, and I am glad it ended up as I predicted. Louise and I have been friends for a long time, not only she works for me, but she has been a good companion since my wife died, our friendship has been wonderful and I hope it will continue forever!"

"Well... there seems to be no end of surprises, I did have a hunch that you didn't look like a chauffeur, however thank you for your good words, I'm so gratefully for all you done for Louise, as far as we are concern you are one of the family now!"

"It was a great pleasure Don, I did enjoy the Champagne, the music and the shows.. incidentally, if you ever need a chauffeur I'll be at your service, mine is waiting outside!"

"Bob won't you stay for another drink..?"

"Don you are so kind, but I presume you'll have a lot to discuss with your lot about your happy reunion, and your new future venture, I wouldn't be surprise.... from a soldier, a kitchen porter, Director accountant, Catering entrepreneur, landlord, and record producer... what next?"

"I have no idea... my hands and mind are full!"

"Take good care of Louise Don, she's a wonderful girl!"

"Rest assure Bob I will!"

"And as for you Louise I wish you many days of happiness, you certainly deserve them!"

"Oh you are a darling Bob, see at the Manor tomorrow!"

"Goodnight Louise and don't be late, we've got so much paper work to sort out in the office, goodnight Don... and goodnight to everyone!"

(Don wants to say a few more words to end the evening)

"Well my friends, now that we have lot of new and old loves reunited, not to forget a new landlady, a daughter and a future son in law, what more could I ask for my birthday? I have now everything, and this is the perfect time to call for a celebration, so the Champagne is on me, wishing you all peace and prosperity!"

"Naturally the celebration is followed by Lisa,the girls and Charlie with their wonderful Charleston; "Love and Champagne"

"All Characters and events of this story, other than those clearly in the public domain are fictitious, and any resemblance to real persons, living or dead are purely coincidental

Words approx; 57,000

The Author

Born in a small town in Northern Italy, Lake Garda. Spent his early days working in Hotels and restaurants in Italy, Switzerland and England. Gained a good knowledge of European languages and an English Diploma at the LTC London School. Always had an ambition of writing songs and stories. In 1959 he wrote his first story called "Princess Snowdrop" Later adapted as a Musical and published on LP records, widely performed in UK schools and in an Italian theatre. Amongst his works he penned many other songs, which were also published on CDs and cassettes by "Sanrocco Music" settled in the region of Kent UK where he opened a successful Italian restaurant. When he doesn't write he enjoys his cooking of Italian and French cuisine for his friends and families.

Giuliano Laffranchi

Printed in Poland
by Amazon Fulfillment
Poland Sp. z o.o., Wrocław